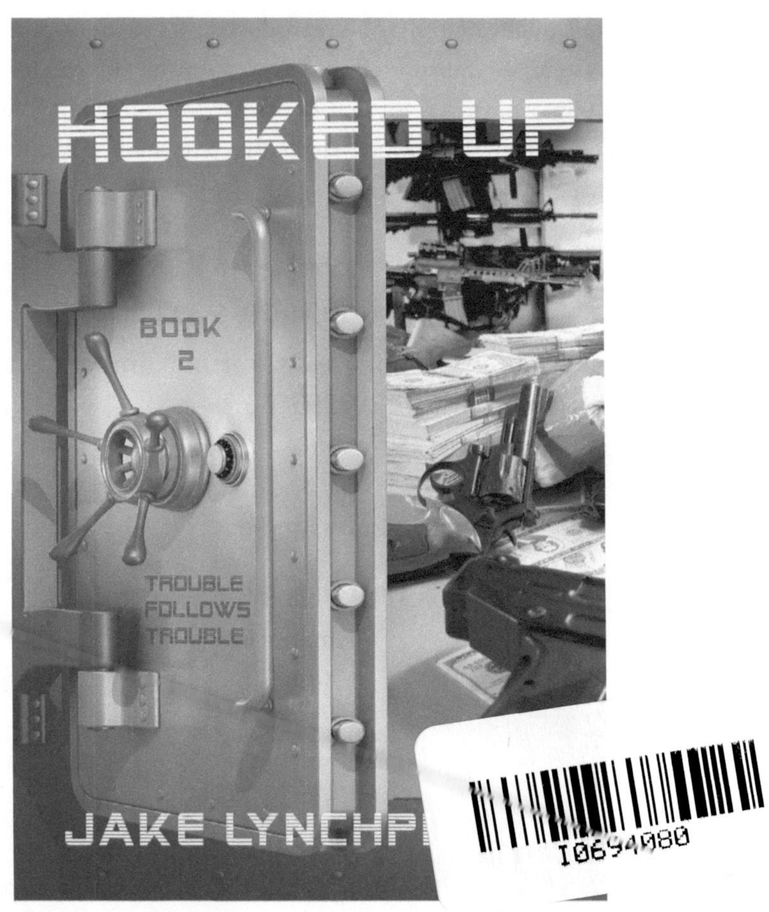

~ Kingpin Press ~

An imprint of

Real

Nice Book

ISBN 979-8-9856670-3-5 Paperback

ISBN 979-8-9856670-4-2 Ebook

Library of Congress Control Number: 2022936867

Published by

~ Kingpin Press ~

An imprint of

Real

Nice Books

11 Dutton Court, Suite 606

Baltimore, Maryland 21228s

www.realnicebooks.com

Publisher's note: The entire contents of this book, including the reviews printed herein, is a work of fiction. Names, characters, places, institutions, and incidents are entirely the product of the author's imagination or are used fictitiously, and any resemblance to actual persons, living or dead, or to events, incidents, institutions, or places is entirely coincidental.

Set in Minion Pro.

Cover photos by ZargonDesign and ShaneQuentin, iStock.com

Also by Jake Lynchpin, Jr.

Hooked Up, Book 1, the first book in the series.

List of Chapters

1

The Long Way Home

Scorp couldn't wait any longer. She was so close. He wanted her.

"Come here." Scorp reached across the massive console of the Chevy Suburban.

Candy hated having sex in vehicles. Cars and trucks had been her "training ground" when she was just a little girl. Her father would take her for special "rides" on Sundays. She shuddered.

"Wait, Scorp, look! See that lady, parked right over there? She needs help. I'll change that flat tire for her and be right back." Candy pointed to the old lady who was peering at her rear tire.

Scorp sighed. "OK, Girl Scout, go for it." Candy, saving someone again. She just couldn't help herself. What was this, the fourth time they'd delayed their trip to help a stranded motorist, homeless person, or stray dog?

Candy approached the older woman, who was leaning against the front fender of her ancient Crown Victoria, staring at her phone. The sun was too bright. She was tilting her phone up, down, and sideways to see the screen. It didn't help. "Hi! Need some help? Looks like you picked up a nail or something, huh?" I can change your tire for you if you want. Won't take long."

The frail, tiny woman took a close look at Candy. She thought Candy had a nice, friendly, gorgeous smile. The shorts this young woman was wearing certainly weren't ideal for changing a tire. At least she wouldn't sweat too much. It was pushing ninety degrees and the humidity was brutal. "You sure you want to do this? I can call my husband. I can't find my Triple A card."

"I'm sure. I've changed plenty of 'em. No need to call your husband. Just take me a few minutes. Open the trunk and I'll get started."

Candy jacked the car up and had the spare tire mounted in ten minutes. "There you go. That should get you home. That spare ain't the best though. Better get all your tires checked soon."

"God bless you, dear. Here, take this." The old lady held out a twenty-dollar bill with a shaky hand and a smile.

Candy backed away and raised her hands. "No way. Don't want that. I have to get back now. Have a safe trip."

Anticipating Candy's return, Scorp put the sunshade up to cover the Suburban's windshield. The twenty-percent window tints on the Suburban took care of the rest. He adjusted the fan setting so the powerful air conditioner wouldn't freeze Candy to death and yanked his sweat pants off.

They'd entered the park-and-ride off Interstate 81, taking a break on their road trip from New Jersey to Tennessee. After changing the tire, Candy climbed back into the Suburban, grabbed a bottle of sanitizer and cleaned her hands with some stray Double Donut napkins. She gulped down a small bottle of ice cold water from the cooler and unrolled a paper towel and swiped it across her forehead. Scorp pulled her top up and over her head. Snap. Zip. Her shorts and panties were off. His seat was back. She straddled him and started working.

Scorp was a good lover, but her feelings for him ran deeper. He'd saved her in more ways than one. He loved it when she acted like a street slut, and Candy always made sure she satisfied that particular desire. The least she could do for the man who was taking her to her new home, in Tennessee, to start over. A brand new life. And after all, street slut was something she knew about. Her father had seen to that. He'd made her, taught her, beat her into acting the part. "Tell me how much you like it baby" while he.... Her father's unpredictable mood swings and uninvited late night visits a part of her past now. No more beatings, sexual assaults, ridiculous expectations, or insane demands coming from her psychopathic dad. Candy and Scorp had waited and planned the escape from her father, known as Manic, for years. It took them what seemed like a lifetime to accumulate enough cash and manage the circumstances needed for their new life together.

No one knew their intention to flee and hook up, back then. Not her father, her friends, or Scorp's "business" associates. Candy wanted Scorp the moment she first laid eyes on his muscled, tattooed arms. They were inked with Scorpions, their tails tangled, meandering from biceps to wrists. She'd been introduced to him while she was still a teen. Scorp was her father's business partner and MMA sparring partner. Scorp knew she was his soulmate within days of their meeting. Smart, beautiful, dangerous. Teaching her Martial Arts at Manic's compound in New Jersey had been so easy. She was a natural. They'd trained and made clandestine love for many weeks at her father's gym, when she was in her teens.

Then, she ran away. Candy couldn't take any more abuse. She could handle most any man with her martial arts skills, but she couldn't handle Manic. Her dad nearly killed her in a savage, sexually fueled rage the night she left her home. Prostitution was her game plan for solitary survival. It wasn't a preference. She had no other skills. No other options. So she settled on that lonely, thankless, dangerous profession. Candy kept in touch with Scorp, texting him daily from motels spanning three states. Scorp stayed behind with Manic in New Jersey, saving all of his substantial earnings. Scorp visited her sporadically over the years whenever he could get away. She'd confided in Scorp. Shared the sick details of her father's sexual obsession with her that started when she was so very young. The beatings. The hardcore sex that left her feeling ashamed and worthless.

Candy managed her chosen profession by using her petite, perfect body. Asset allocation at its best. Scorp invested in double D size breasts for Candy. Twelve five for the best. They looked real. Felt real. She worked motels near Annapolis. She tried to work with other girls for safety and company. The men who visited? She just wanted them gone. Quickly. Every aspect of her profession sickened her, but it was her only recourse. She easily handled the occasional problem client. No man could intimidate or manhandle her. She'd make them pay in pain and suffering. Go home and explain those bruises to your wife, asshole. There weren't any vacations or sick days. She was twenty-four seven and advertised so. If she wanted the money, she had to make herself available. It wasn't her schedule to set. Her schedule was set by her clients. She had some "regulars." They were a safer bet, but also tried to get "close" sometimes. Candy didn't encourage that behavior. It wasn't productive. Wasted far too much time. She sent padded envelopes stuffed with cash to Scorp's P.O. box monthly. All the money she made except living expenses and various nineteen-dollar-a-month payments to animal rights groups, child care hospitals, and wounded warrior projects went to Scorp . The cash flow was phenomenal at times, especially when conventions were scheduled in Baltimore or Annapolis. That money, and Scorp's massive paychecks from working car theft and strong arm jobs with her father added up. And then, to top it off, Candy took her naïve dentist David for a financial spin. She'd upped her body-for-hire ante with David. The cars, cash, credit cards, watches, and jewelry she stole from him surpassing months of lower level sex work earnings. Candy didn't consider it grand larceny. David the dentist eventually figured out what was happening and allowed it. After all, he was getting what he wanted too. He'd talked about his sexless marriage with his money grubbing realtor wife. Candy showed him what he'd been missing. It had been so easy. So easy, she felt a twinge of regret that she had taken so much from him. In her heart, she knew David wasn't a bad guy. It was easier taking advantage of the scores of men buying her favors who were disgusting, easy-to-hate men. She'd also scored a full set of brilliant white teeth from David. Her smile, once missing a front tooth, had been transformed into movie star level perfection. She missed David sometimes. He talked to her, about her. Not himself. David could sense what she really wanted. To be accepted.

Her father's threatening hold on Scorp kept him from joining her all those desperate years. And Scorp hated the occasional job her father took which required him to maim or kill. He hadn't signed up for that and wasn't a willing participant. Manic didn't seem to mind killing. Part of his nature, he thought. All those problems were solved now. Scorp never shared the details of Manic's demise with Candy. He did arrive in Annapolis and show her the body. Her dad's neck broken, his head twisted backwards. She'd shed exactly one single solitary tear when she saw his lifeless body, then smiled. And now, the dead man could have no influence on her. Or, maybe…? Candy was surprised that Scorp had been able to overpower and kill her father. Manic was beyond the typical ba-dass. He'd been competitive in professional UFC bouts. She never asked what led to their fight. She didn't want to know the details. Maybe now the nightmares would end? The ones where she woke up screaming in terror, dreaming Manic was on top of her, inside her, his hot breath on her neck. If she had just had a mother. A mother would've protected her. If her mother hadn't disappeared when she was two, maybe things would've been different.

Candy dressed and they exited the park-and-ride, back on 81 South, towards Tennessee. Scorp's neck and face were flushed. She'd done well. He was satisfied, for now.

"Did they finish up the vault, Scorp?" Scorp had ordered an actual bank vault for installation underground at their new house in Tennessee.

"Yeah, they texted pics. It's done."

"And you had your guys move the shit in an' lock it?"

"Yeah, babe. It's all done. You'll see it soon enough."

They arrived at their destination. Great Smoky Mountains. Seclusion. Exclusive. Fifteen acres surrounding the five-bedroom six-bath retreat. Mountain top. Three million. They'd paid that in cash to construct their new home. Compared to New Jersey real estate prices it was a bargain. Candy had to be talked into moving. Tennessee? She liked Maryland and New Jersey. Hadn't been many other places. New York on a call girl job once. Scorp convinced her to move to Tennessee. He described it as safe and secure. Those words held weight with her.

Scorp pulled his new SUV into the six-car garage. Elevator down. The elevator door opened up to a wide underground hallway leading to the vault. An unusual feature for a residence, but not unheard of. The vault walls were three inches thick. Candy had questioned that. She didn't think that was thick enough.

"Scorp, that three inches doesn't seem to be very thick. I thought vaults were like, three feet thick? Like, anybody could get past three inches, right?"

"It's special concrete, Candy. It's got stainless steel on top of it. It'd be tough to get in. Them old vaults were thicker, but not as strong."

"What would it take for somebody to crack it, Scorp?"

"I asked about that. They'd need a burner bar torch. I think that's what it's called. Burns liquid oxygen. Real hot. Something like eight thousand degrees. Might work, not sure. But ain't nobody gonna try that on our vault anyway when they don't even know what's in it. And I'm not planning on tellin' anybody what's in it, are you?"

"Why would I tell anybody? Besides, who am I gonna tell? I don't have anybody except you, and you already know. A special torch? Hmm...."

Vault locks normally took two people to open. Scorp had those specifications changed so that it only took one person. He felt more comfortable knowing that either he or Candy could get in without the other. He nixed the standard time lock feature also. Other than those two deleted items, it was the same vault specification used by Bank of U.S.A. It took eight weeks for the vault to be manufactured, shipped, and installed below ground level at their house. Scorp was assured that it would be nearly impossible to break into. Skids of cash, weapons, jewelry, and drugs were stored inside. Enough cash for a lifetime behind the vault door. Scorp and Candy did not trust traditional banks. And cash deposits in large amounts would raise suspicion. Cash *on hand* soothed them. Their house had been bought through a shell Corporation. Out-of-state contractors and confidentiality agreements signed to insured their secrets stayed secret. Their house and vault were essentially off the grid.

Scorp entered the combination, opened the vault and placed his travel weapons carefully in the foam lined stainless steel cases. Then they took inventory. Using a box cutter, Scorp quickly removed the shrink wrap and cardboard, and Candy moved the trash out of the vault. The vault smelled like fresh minted money and marijuana. He handed his phone to her. It held the inventory list. They checked what they could, for now. They'd use a bill counter to be sure, later.

"Looks good, Candy. Everything's here. Here…some spendin' money." He'd stuffed bundles of hundred-dollar bills into a backpack and handed it to her. Scorp swung the immense vault door shut behind them on the way out.

"Thanks," she said. She wasn't inclined to say thanks. The way he'd *said* that—"spending money." Like it was *his* money. Were all men the same? Was she just a convenience with no real value? She'd been responsible for a big chunk of the vault's contents. But they'd just arrived, she was tired, and in no mood to fight. Let it go… just let it go…for now.

"What's through those other doors, Scorp?" Candy hadn't noticed doors on either side of the hall when she'd reviewed and edited the house plans. She was positive they weren't represented. She walked down to get a closer look.

"Oh, that's a utility room. Scorp pointed to the door on the left side. "See, look…it's marked."

As Candy drew close, she saw a small metal sign. It read Mechanical Room. Satisfied, she turned to the door on the opposite side of the hallway, another ten feet further down. "What about that door. That wasn't on the plans either. Where does it go? What's it for?"

"That's a tool room."

"Tool room? A whole room? For tools?"

"Yeah, well, some trade tools and equipment for jobs. Don't need them to be takin' up room in the vault. They're worth a lot of money. I want them to be secure, you know? There's a key to it up on the door molding. I'll set up a key box for all our locks soon."

Elevator two floors up. They threw their bags down in the living room and headed to the oversized owner's suite. Scorp tossed her on their California king bed. He threw Candy's clothes across the room. She reached for him. He swatted her hand away.

"Oh Scorp, c'mon! Oh…my…God." He pinned her down and placed his hand across her throat….

In the morning, Candy was up first, and sauntered around the house. The house plans and pictures the contractors had sent them paled in comparison to the real thing. The house and furnishings were extraordinary. The interior designer they had hired filled the rooms perfectly. They gave him free reign and a blank check. Candy and Scorp had no experience with the finer things in life.

They were rested. In the new house for a few months now. Matching terry robes. Coffee on the deck. Late fall. Slight chill in the air. Candy's thoughts drifted to the rough romps with Scorp. Curious. With Scorp, she liked it a *little* rough. Was she programmed that way? Could it be that her father's rough…? No…no. And that unaccounted for room near the vault? What was that all about? She didn't think tools needed their own room with a steel door that looked impenetrable. Soon her thoughts and questions returned to the present and future. Doldrums had arrived. Boredom never served her well. Problematic. The life she'd waited and saved for now a reality. Her man with her. But her restlessness was pervasive. Time slowing down to a slow crawl of…nothing.

Scorp didn't talk. She'd liked that, at first. She'd never lived with a man. Her father didn't count. Living with Scorp was *different*. He did the same thing every day. Up at dawn. Ran three miles. Worked out. Washed up. Woke her up. Worked her over. She missed the true intimacy she'd shared with her old girlfriend,

Gina. Gina, her lover, workmate and confidant. Gina was her motel roommate. They'd met at the Bedtime Six motel, near Annapolis, and quickly became best friends. Now Gina's whereabouts were uncertain. Candy missed the late night snuggletalks with Gina. She longed for the cash flow rush when they ran doubles up 95 towards Philly. The drug fueled sex she'd experienced with Gina was etched in her memory. Neighbors, Syd and Audrey, who lived across the cul-de-sac from them, had befriended Gina and offered her lodging. Seems the wife talked her husband into it. Claimed Gina's child wouldn't survive without their help. Good for Gina, Candy thought. Maybe Gina was happy living with them? The family she never had? Did Gina miss Candy's touch? Candykisses? She wanted to text, to talk to Gina. But, no number. No email addy. No luck. She'd work on that. But how to contact her, other than just driving back to Annapolis? She wasn't doing that. Not without talking to Gina first. She wanted to ask Scorp for help contacting her, but he was way too busy right now. And she sensed he was jealous of Gina. He'd never said anything, but Candy was positive he could see her intense arousal that Gina's nude body caused when they were in bed. If she could just see her again. She'd even welcome Gina's daughter, Lily. The daughter who'd eventually come between her and Gina, stealing Gina's time and affection.

"Would you mind if I searched up a companion, Scorp ? A female? You know, maybe somebody like…Gina? Keep me company when you're out on a job?" She reached. Touched. Scorp couldn't be read. *Impossible.* Except when jacked up by sex, or violence. He didn't react to her question, or touch. She lit a Newport and watched the chilly breeze adjust the smoke. Scorp was distant, as usual. Preoccupied. He was usually either in the garage, or pacing the driveway with a burner. May as well live alone, she thought.

"Sure, Candy. Would be good to make some friends, huh? Just be careful."

Permission? She didn't need permission. Just made sense to ask. He knew her, right? Knew she liked the feel, touch, and taste of a woman. He'd rolled with her and Gina—an Ecstasy fueled orgy about nine months ago. He'd watched her with Gina. Up close. Shared his hard body with both of them. Candy's bisexuality was not an issue with Scorp. So why did she feel a twinge when she asked the question? Guilt? Fear? Not sure. Not going to fret though. Not now. He'd said sure. Good enough.

"Okay, Scorp. Let's go in. Gettin' chilly. An' thanks. I'll make sure whoever I find likes men too."

"Humph."

She was always somewhat amused. Scorp had no idea what a sexual treasure he was. He lasted just the right length of time. Eight to ten minutes. And his natural toughness? He didn't try to stifle it. Wouldn't be able to anyway. He'd please any woman. Those that were stunned initially ended up craving more. She'd witnessed that.

It was daybreak. Candy was up with him. Showered with him. Dried him off. Got him off. Saw him off. His Suburban packed and headed out. Candy stayed behind. Scorp liked the action. The irreplaceable rush of a big-time car theft. Money rewards not a concern. Cover expenses and make a little spending money. And bond with crew. As much as he could bond. Which wasn't much. All the inner workings of any steal-deal by way of the dark web. Information on exotic car locations for sale to the highest bidder were listed there, and Scorp was a regular bidder. He'd "inherited" Candy's dad's car business, and enhanced it. Never a presence near the target area. Safe. No mistakes, ever. Mistakes like the dead State Trooper Manic shot in haste during their final job together. No rental cars to trace. No local yokel helpers. He'd be gone awhile. The cars he'd targeted were halfway across the country.

Scorp was confident about his business. He wasn't as confident he could keep Candy happy. He knew her, yet he didn't. He didn't need a social atmosphere. He only needed his Candy. She, however, seemed restless. Seclusion was ideal for him. He needed it. Candy? He wasn't sure she would handle it well, or at all. She was used to constant daily action, even if it wasn't necessary, or safe. He'd seen her in action with Gina. The cocaine, molly, heroin, and percocets they'd shared contributing to their lifestyle of mayhem. He thought Candy might settle down, with Manic and Gina no longer in the mix. *Maybe….*

Candy's dilemma? She was lonely. Bored and lonely. The idea of living with Scorp was so appealing she hadn't given any thought to how she would fill the void when he was away working. No Gina to share her innermost thoughts. No clients to mess with. If Scorp would just listen to her. Talk to her about anything besides sex, cars, and money. She knew no one in the town, or the entire state. The local women? She'd tried to connect. Pretty enough. Nice enough. Southern. Loved their accents. Somewhat generic look, though. Like they all texted each other before getting dressed. Same hair styles, shoes. She tried flirtshopping. Asking for assistance, trying on outfits when she found a hot retail babe. Eyeflirts, show a little skin, maybe a touch? Nothing worked. Could her Jersey accent be a turnoff? Maybe she'd do a tourist tour? People from all over the country came here on vacation, but she wanted something steady, not a one nighter. Somebody to connect with emotionally. Who "got" her. But Candy's new hood was a family destination. Mini golf, minivans, and zip lines. Not conducive to Candy's needs. And she wasn't going to church. She wasn't that desperate, yet. That seemed to be the main event. She'd never seen so many churches. Everywhere. Like bars in Jersey. One on every corner. There must be something to it?

2

Ladies Night

One nightclub advertised in the local paper she'd resigned herself to attempt to read. The ad was at the bottom of the back page, below an article about three women found raped and murdered in the last few months. The women described were all young blondes between eighteen and twenty-four. The club depicted in the quarter-page ad was not a true nightclub, Candy thought. Looked like it was actually a restaurant with a second floor bar and dance floor. Worth a try? It was that or another night alone. Netflix binges alone on the couch weren't cutting it. And she had no clue when Scorp would be back. Maybe she could hook up.

She blow dried her hair. Longer now. Scorp liked it long. Easy to gather up and pull. What to wear? Not wanting to stand out, too much. Conservative. Not too tight jeans. High boots. Loose, thin upscale hoodie. Underneath, a red and black flannel shirt. Countrified. She'd take the new Odyssey. Beige blend in. She hated the van. Scorp *insisted* that she drive a van. Her beloved Challenger SRT8 was to sit covered in the garage. She wasn't to drive it in town. No attention. No flair. Soccer mom front. Scorp said they must hide their wealth and their past. Her thoughts drifting back to the times cruising with Gina in the Challenger, causing near accident distractions, everywhere they went. David the dentist had bought the car for her. She loved the power, the flash. The van? Just another symbol of suburban stagnation. But she *had to try*. Drive a minivan. Try to change. Become that person who could be trusted. Have good friends, without strings.

She was a half block away from the club. Too many tourists. Trivago twits, she thought. Sidewalk strollers window shopping after dinner. Not many though. It was after 9 p.m. Past bedtime in vacationland. She lit a Newport as she made her way to the club. Nobody smoked in this town. What was with these people? Alive? She thought not. Zombie dead with two point five kids and a mortgage. Men were afraid to acknowledge her. Turning away as she approached. Her magnificent high dollar implants wasted here. Wife conscious. Just as well, she thought. Random men were no longer needed for income, and these people looked *happy*. Maybe she could fit in. Be happy.

She crossed the street to Club 654. It wasn't much. But right now? All she had. Scorp gone for who knew how long. Their new house? Big. Quiet. Lonely. The acreage seeing to it that there weren't any houses within sight. Not a streetlight or sidewalk for miles. No sounds. Except the nighttime nature noises that kept her up, wondering what kind of animal that was and how close it was, and bird choruses during the day. She took the stairs on the side of the redwood building to the second-floor entrance to the club. There she found a fake stained glass double door opening to a paneled foyer and a second set of glass doors.

The doorman stopped her, asked for identification. She'd left that at the house.

"I'm sorry. I don't have it with me. I'm almost twenty-four." The doorman was maybe twenty. Very cute, she thought. He was having a tough time maintaining eye contact.

"Sorry, Ma'am. I need to see something. It's not my rules." This was the young doorman's second job he'd taken to make ends meet. Couldn't afford to make mistakes. He needed this gig.

"Need to see something, huh? Might be able to arrange that. You're cute, and I'm alone tonight. Could you walk me to my car when I leave?" He held the door for her. Candy winked. Everyone makes mistakes. She was in.

Candy surveyed the room. Way too bright. And way too many eyes on her. She walked along the perimeter of the dance floor and made her way to the ladies room. Hoodie off and her flannel shirt unbuttoned, three down. That's all she'd need. The bathroom door flew open, almost hitting her on the way out. A pretty blonde brushed by and flung a stall door open, turning.

"Oh, honey, I'm so sorry. I didn't see you." Candy's first three minutes not going well.

Candy made her way to the bar. Feeling out of place. Needed a drink. Now.

"Grey Goose on the rocks." The ponytailed, scruffy bartender smiled and turned to get her drink. There were two older men seated apart from the numerous couples at the bar. They were having an alcohol enhanced high volume conversation. She picked up her drink, moved down, and sat next to them.

"Hi guys. How ya doing tonight? You from around here, or visiting?"

Their conversation halted. Two gray heads turning towards her in unison. One replying. "Yeah, we live here. You don't look or sound like you're from around here, though. Right?"

"Nah, from Jersey. Down here visiting a friend. He left for a few days. So, thought I'd check out this place."

"I have to head home, Jim. Talk to you soon." One gray head gone. One left.

Candy could smell whiskey on Jim's breath as he leaned in. Late forties? Hard to tell. Tanned. Handsome. Huge bronzed hands. No wedding ring. Broad shoulders. He might ease her mind temporarily? She could close her eyes tight and pretend those strong hands were Scorp's? Whisper how much she wanted it? But she didn't want trouble. Just some simple fun. She'd even tell Scorp if she strayed. He wouldn't expect she could settle down completely in the little time they'd been there, she told herself. She couldn't remember the last time she was this alone. It wasn't comfortable.

"Name's Candise. Call me Candy. And you're…Jim?"

"Yeah, Jim. Nice to meet you, Candy." He offered his hand. Her tiny hand was surprisingly firm. She squeezed. He felt a finger stroke his palm. Candy held on.

"Buy me a drink, Jim?" She'd finished her first with four quick gulps.

"Why of course. My pleasure."

Fresh Grey Goose appeared in front of her. Candy was feeling better. Her hand found his upper thigh. Soft, short strokes. She stood and brushed her breasts against his shoulder, then pressed lightly, gauging his reaction. She turned and leaned against the bar. He seemed like a nice guy. He might even *talk*.

"Jim, what do you do? Your hands are *so* rough. Construction?"

"Have a business. Outside of town. Equipment rental. I've lived here my whole life. This town is, well…let's say…not much going on. Kinda boring, really. How about you, Candy?"

"I'm sort of retired, I guess you could say. Lucked into a little money. Thought this area might be a nice change from Jersey, so I'm spending some time here. Checkin' it out. It's a change all right. And not really a good one, so far. Maybe we could hang out tonight, Jim? Make it more interesting?"

Unexpected. An innocent drink with a friend turns into a tiny hot blonde interested in him. Her hand on his thigh. Stirrings he hadn't felt for eons. Jim had never married. He wasn't active with the women in town. Too much responsibility with the business to take on even more, with a woman. He had to focus on his business. The business wouldn't take care of him, or his parents, who were in assisted living, if he didn't give it his full attention. Right now though? Candy had his full attention. He placed a hand atop hers.

"I didn't have any plans for tonight, but I do now, Jim. Let's finish our drinks and head over to my friend's place. Get to know each other. Have a few drinks. The house is real nice…an' real private."

"I'll have to take a raincheck, Candy. I need to be up early." He said auditors from the bank would be at his office in the morning. As much as he wanted to stay and get to know this pretty young woman, he needed to be on time tomorrow and extra alert to answer their questions. They had inventory inquiries, and God only knew what other questions he would have to answer. His business was in jeopardy. The other meetings he had lined up weren't going to be pleasant either.

"You gotta be kidding!" Candy blurted out. A first. A male turning her down for sleep? Did this guy think he was something special? Had fairy dust shooting out of his penis? This town. These people. A willing girl right next to him itching to be scratched and he needs his beauty sleep? Did she need to spell it out for him?

"Wish I was kidding. I have important meetings tomorrow morning. I'm real sorry, Candy. I come here around this time a few times a week. Maybe we'll see each other again." He swallowed the last of his drink and stood up to leave.

"Wait, give me your number, Jim. I'll text you, so you'll have mine."

"Why sure. You can call or text any time, Candy. I'd sure like to chat some more."

Candy entered Jim's number as he left, saved it as a contact, finished her drink, and made her way around the dance floor. She needed to make a quick bathroom stop on the way out. She'd seen enough of the 654 for tonight. Still reeling from the conversation with Jim. She must be getting old? Or maybe it was the flannel shirt? Just when she needed someone to talk to, other than Scorp. Finishing up, she leaned over the sink for a facial close up. Nothing out of place. She smiled. Her high dollar dental work was still intact and brilliant. What was wrong? Maybe it was for the best, she thought. She would have to get comfortable being alone. Find friends that didn't want her body.

The bathroom door swung open. Candy looked up. The blonde from earlier. Their eyes met briefly in the mirror. Candy was washing her hands. The woman went in the stall directly behind her. Stall door left open. Jeans squiggled down a bit. Her top riding up. Sliver of the top of red panties visible. Pierced belly button. Defined stomach. Their eyes met in the mirror. The stall door closed.

"You like what you saw?" Voice over stall. Candy was drying her hands.

"Yeah, I sure did. You wanna hang out with me? This place sucks. I'm leavin'. Meet me outside?" At this point, Candy wasn't going to be picky. And this this woman, from the little she'd seen, was attractive, and fit. And women usually liked to *talk*. She'd take a chance. What could it hurt?

"Yeah, sounds great. I'll be right out." She had spotted Candy the minute she walked through the doors to the club. She watched her chat up the older guys at the bar. Seemed to be confident and outgoing. She wasn't going to pass up a chance to get to know her.

They met on the upper landing, outside the club. The shy young doorman noticed the little blonde he'd helped get in earlier chatting up the woman he'd seen in the club a few times before. Glance and smile. He'd seen the taller blonde leaving with out-of-town women once or twice since he'd been working there. She'd never so much as looked at him. There was something about her….

"Name's Candy. You're real pretty. What's your name?" Candy moved closer.

"My name is Jo. Thanks, and, you know, I really enjoyed seeing you bent over the sink. You're cute, Candy."

"Well, thanks! Hey, Jo, look, I owe that guy a favor. She pointed to the young doorman. He helped me out earlier. Forgot my ID and he let me in anyways. You wanna take him with us?" Candy motioned to him. "We can all party at my friend's house. Might be fun? Ain't far."

"Why not. He's been staring at me every time I've come here. I guess he's harmless and he's not bad looking. He's definitely awkward. I've seen him fumble and stumble checking IDs a few times."

Candy walked over to him. "How about takin' a ride with us, dude? Hang out with us tonight."

"Sorry, I can't leave. Don't get off until two, and then I have to help clean up."

"Well, that's a real shame. You sure? You look like you might be getting sick, and we'd like the company. I've got a nice place pretty close by. Got some 420 if you care to…what's your name?

I'm Candy and this is Jo."

"Erik…nice to meet you both." Was this happening? Two hot blondes asking him to go home with them? It wasn't a difficult decision.

3

Uncertainty

Scorp had done it a hundred times, or more. What was at one time complicated, now simple. Learning curve transformed into muscle memory. The years working with Candy's father had prepared him well. The business he helped Manic grow was now all his. *He* was in charge. The underground exotic car market had exploded in recent years. Stock market gains were being plowed into hard assets for protection and appreciation. The market was worldwide. Scorp knew the players, the product, and the profit margins. No, he didn't need the money. It wasn't that. The *challenge*. That was what drove him. But there was a persistent voice inside that kept growing louder, cajoling him to consider retiring. Marry Candy. Start a family. Enjoy the fruits of his dangerous, difficult work.

Scorp had seriously considered staying home with Candy. Canceling the project to be with her. He was concerned about her on several fronts. She'd told him she wanted to look for a woman, a companion, to ease her loneliness while he was working. Would she find a woman and fall in love while he was working? A woman like Gina? He thought he fulfilled Candy's sexual needs, but wasn't positive. She'd been with so many, many men. Yes, she was "working" with those men, but still….And then the parties with Gina. He'd seen them together and it wasn't something he could duplicate. He didn't have a woman's body, or touch. He'd overheard their conversations filled with emotion and feeling. Not his strong suit. Candy reacted differently with a woman. He didn't feel threatened by Candy's bisexuality. He just couldn't compete. And with her male clients? He had no idea. It wasn't something he or Candy would ever bring up for discussion. Off limits.

The drugs in the vault were another potential problem. Candy had quit. Or so she'd told him. Dugs no longer a driving force in her life. Just like her father was dead, her drug use was dead. The vault at their new house contained enough drugs to stoke Candy's fire for a decade. He'd resisted her purchases, but she assured him it was a good investment. She'd sell all of the stored drugs at a tremendous profit. "No biggie," he was told. Scorp wasn't sure. And now he'd be away from her, with a return date that wasn't firm. So he'd decided to change the combination to the underground vault before he left. Candy had enough cash in the backpack he'd given her to last months without visiting the cash skids in the vault. When he got back home, he'd change the combination back and Candy would never know. Then he'd have another talk with her about the drugs. He didn't think the risk of possessing was worth the reward. And there was a bigger risk. Candy using. Her heavy cocaine use in the past harmed her and their savings. She'd only used heroin a few times that he knew of, but then again that's just what she'd told him. She never had track marks, or abscesses, but Scorp knew there were soft ways of doing heroin. Up the nose, or butt. That would be harder to detect. Heroin wasn't recreational. And there were six kilos of heroin in the vault, along with bricks of coke and weed. The street value of the heroin alone was over a million. Not insignificant, but he'd burn it all in a heartbeat if it became a problem. They'd come too far.

And then the "other door" that led to a tool and equipment storage area. Candy had a *look* when she thought she was being lied to. He recognized it. Her head would tilt just a bit to the left and a smile would be just barely detectable. He'd seen it a hundred times. Not something she could cover up. Scorp planned on showing her the tool room at some point. He just wasn't ready and was embarrassed that he wouldn't be able to explain it very well. Bottom line? He should have made a stronger effort disguising the entrance.

He'd think things through and figure everything out by the

time he returned home. Right now, he had to clear his mind, and focus on the task at hand.

4

Missing Person

"Where's Erik? Did he leave? Catch an Uber?" Candy and Jo were up and having coffee in the kitchen as Candy asked the question. It was 8 a.m. Way too early for Candy to be up. She hadn't slept well, waking up and reliving her life, unable to stop the video replay taking place in her head.

"I have no idea where he is, Candy. When I woke up a little while ago, he wasn't in the living room. I thought he might be with…." She stopped short and lowered her eyes.

"I slept alone, Jo. My door was locked."

At Club 654 the night before, they'd convinced Erik to join them. He'd feigned a stomach issue as Candy had suggested, and the club's owner let him go for the night. Candy asked him to drive. Erik agreed. He would have done anything she asked him to do. He was going to be all alone with *them*. He remembered the last time he was alone with a woman. How it felt. He looked into the rearview mirror and gave himself a smile. And this time there were *two*.

"Set the nav to 'home,' Erik." They were in Candy's Odyssey. "I'm gonna ride back here with Jo." Candy was hoping Jo could help her. Someone to chat with, shop with and confide in. Talk to! A girlfriend. Erik was fumbling. He hated navigation systems. They were all different. And now he'd have to ask a girl show him how it worked. Embarrassing, at best.

"Here, let me help you." Candy swung her leg over the console. Erik could smell her perfume. Her shirt was partially unbuttoned. He caught a glimpse as she leaned over. She turned to face him and smiled. Perfect pouty lipsticked lips. And her teeth were awesome. He had that overpowering, familiar feeling. The mixture of emotions he'd felt so many times before. His mind was calculating feverishly. Calm down, he told himself. In due time….

Candy kissed him on the cheek. "There ya' go, Erik. That'll get us there."

Candy climbed back to her seat, and lit a Newport. "Want one, Jo?"

"Nah, don't smoke."

"Erik?"

"No thanks."

Candy was attracted. Jo had a gorgeous, clear, porcelain complexion. Short, spiky, trendy blonde hair. Perfect makeup. Just right jewelry. Crisp clothes. A wispy red scarf. Big green eyes. She was thin, somewhat tall, and graceful. Nails to die for. Sultry, sexy voice. Her arms were thin and toned. Her smile was near Candy-bright. She smelled great. And so calm. Candy was intrigued. Jo was "different."

"Where did you grow up, Jo. Around here?"

"D.C., New York, we moved around…you?"

"Jersey. Most people know once I say something."

"Drive through the gates and pull into the garage, Erik." Candy opened the gates surrounding the property and garage door remotely.

"Who the heck lives here, Candy? Elon Musk?" Jo was impressed. She'd only seen houses like this in magazines. The custom paver driveway? She estimated a hundred thousand, at least. Candy didn't fit the image of a girl who had friends with this kind of money. Jo was surprised, and it must have shown. Erik hadn't said a word.

Candy looked at Jo. " Who's that? Elon Must? No, Jo, it belongs to a friend. He's in the car business. A dealer. High end shit. I can't even like, say the names of some of those cars he sells. He's got a couple houses." Candy led them to the elevator that was in a nook on the far wall of the garage. Erik watched the way their hips swayed and listened to their small talk. "Goin' up!" The elevator door opened up to the main level foyer.

"Oh my! This place is…really, really, nice!" Jo tilted her head and twirled, taking it all in.

Beyond first class, she thought. A professional had designed Candy's friend's place.

"Your friend has great taste, Candy. Wow…I love it!"

"Got Wi-Fi?" Erik interrupted.

"Sure, Erik. Password is Candyland."

"Sit. Get comfortable." She'd led them into the living room. Candy tried to set the mood. She adjusted the lighting and lit two candles.

"What can I get you two to drink?"

"A beer if you got it." Erik was fidgety, scrolling on his phone. He hadn't put it down or even looked up.

"I'll have the same, Candy." Jo fingered her scarf, adjusting it.

"Anything else? I've got some killer diesel weed, or four star white lady?"

Jo and Erik glanced at each other nervously. Jo spoke up. "I don't do drugs."

"Me neither, Candy."

"Oh…OK, no problem. I'll be right back with your drinks."

Candy took the elevator down to the lowest level, one floor down from the garage. She unlocked the outer door that led to the vault, then entered the combination. Beep. She tried again. Beep. And again. Beep. She'd promised Scorp she wouldn't use, but she just wanted to retrieve enough herb for a joint and just a little coke. Just tonight, then she'd stop again, like she'd promised. The vault combination wasn't working. She locked up the entrance door and picked out a six pack of Heineken from the refrigerator on her way back to her guests. She'd deal with the combination another day. And anyway, this would be a good test. Sex without drugs.

Jo wanted to play a board game, or cards. Candy didn't have a single board game. The only game she played was Candy Crush, on her phone. And she didn't play cards very well. Well, not at all. Erik suggested watching a movie. Candy handed him the remote and sat between them. Erik picked a chick flick on Netflix, then went back to his phone. He was smiling and texting someone. They settled in. Shoes off. Comfy.

Candy rested her hand on Jo's leg, gingerly. Jo moved it off, gently, looking Candy squarely in the eye. "Let's watch the movie, Candy. This is supposed to be really good."

Candy was feeling down. It didn't make sense. Jo had enticed her earlier, and now she wanted to watch a movie? Maybe she shouldn't have invited Erik? Was Jo shy around guys? She'd agreed to him coming. It didn't add up. The entire evening a complete disaster. She was mentally exhausted. First the nice looking older man Jim at the 654 needing sleep, then the combination to the vault not working, and now Jo putting her off. And Erik? He was nodding off after his second beer.

Candy left them. They'd both fallen asleep on the sofa, half-way through the movie. She went off to her bedroom. At least her nightstand friend wouldn't let her down. She stripped, found her friend, spread her legs, and sighed. The batteries were dead. Maybe tonight was some sort of sign? An omen? A message it was time to change? After all, she wasn't a street girl anymore. She should stop acting like one. She was so used to using men, women, couples, everyone, for her own benefit. Manipulation. Sexual traps. Blackmail. When anyone was attracted, she saw profit. She wasn't desperate anymore. Wanted real friends. Not "friends" who paid her to do things their wife or girlfriends wouldn't do. She wanted to make love, not perform. Even now, as good as things were with her lover Scorp, she had to roleplay for him. Not that it was difficult, but it wasn't real. Lacking batteries, she improvised, and fell asleep.

"Yeah, bring your coffee, Jo. Let's see if he's in one of the bedrooms."

Candy and Jo checked every room in the house. Erik was gone.

Not a sign he'd ever been there, or slept there, except for two empty beer bottles and creases in the sofa where he'd slept.

"Ok Jo, he's not here. Let's take a break and talk. And give me your number, Jo."

"Sure. Guess I have some explaining to do."

5

Overdue

Scorp was always on time—never late. Ever. Something must have happened. His crew was worried. Not worried about Scorp's welfare. Worried that he screwed them. Did he arrange the sale of the cars, hire them to steal them, only to keep their share of the profits? He owed them four hundred seventy-five grand. The stolen exotic cars were in transit to the Port of Wilmington. Scorp typically used that port to ship stolen exotics, in containers. This plan was no different from last time, or the time before that. They'd meet Scorp after their job was finished. He'd pay them in cash. They'd been waiting two hours. Waiting patiently to be paid wasn't something they did.

Scorp's two crew members, Abe and Jamey, were nervous. They talked options. It'd now been four hours. No word from Scorp. They were convinced he'd decided to sell the cars and keep all of the profit.

"That blonde he's been hanging with probably had a hand in this, Jamey. What did he call her? Candy?" They were pouring over all the possibilities as to why Scorp might be late. "We never had any problems until he hooked up permanent with her. I knew she was trouble. She fuckin' pussy whipped Scorp. Damn pussies got all the power. I'd sooner just jerk off than put up with all that bull-shit comes with women. Bet she talked him into keeping our fee." Abe didn't share his partner Jamey's universal attraction to the opposite sex. Abe viewed women as obstacles to success.

They'd been drinking and thinking for hours. Thoughts and fears. Would he try to kill them? Eliminate the threat of reprisal? He'd know they'd come after him. Scorp knew them well enough. Knew they'd be looking tirelessly to recover their share of the money and punish him. They'd laughed with him over beers before. How Abe handled the occasional "problems" with their side of the business. Capture, torture, maim, murder. Pretty simple stuff. Scorp would be looking over his shoulder, or coming after them, first. They'd need to prepare for action.

"Jamey, we need a plan. We can't wait too long. Keep calling his burner tonight. If he don't answer us by morning, time's up." I say we take one finger for each hundred thousand he shorted us."

"Sounds good, Abe. Hard to believe he stiffed us, but it sure looks that way. If he did, his girlfriend will suffer, too. She's gonna wish she never met him. Bet you got some body surgery in mind for her after we make her air tight." Jamey had to talk tough like that to ensure Abe's respect. He'd never hurt anyone intentionally. His partner Abe was the sociopath. The times that they needed to strong-arm anyone? Jamey always made excuses to avoid being part of it. He just wanted his money.

Scorp had a routine. He'd be in place to monitor Abe and Jamey's progress at the theft site remotely. Make sure they didn't mess up. Or steal an extra car for themselves. He always paid for an additional team to set up live video, so he would watch the job unfold from his SUV. He ate and slept in the back of his Suburban. No motels or purchases. No electronic trail. Always at least a hundred miles away. Then, when he was satisfied the stolen cars were secure and in transit, he'd make his way to the designated meeting spot and pay them for their efforts. As perfect as he could make it. And it'd always been perfect.

The 1962 Ferrari 250 GTO, 1970 Porsche 917K and 1992 McLaren F1, with a street value totaling ninety-five million dollars were being loaded into an enclosed car carrier, headed for Wilmington, Delaware. From there, a container ship would transport them to their destination, Dubai. Export required that certificate of title be submitted seventy-two hours before export. Scorp had those documents forged and delivered three days ago. Scorp turned off his monitor. Just a few more hours and he'd head back to Candy and his mountain home. He missed Candy. She had a presence. He'd become used to her being with him. And in bed she was…*awesome*. Whatever he wanted or needed. Every day, even three times if he wanted. She could keep up. And it was nice having a woman living with him. A first. He liked her sleeping with him, scratching his back and she'd even started microwaving a meal occasionally. They were starting to be a regular type citizen couple. Not bad for two street people who'd never committed to anyone. No one. Ever.

He never used the navigation in the Suburban. Paranoia. Didn't think it was wise should anyone ever retrieve the addresses stored in the memory. So he entered the destination in his phone and placed it in the dash holder. The money drop point was about 125 miles away. Rest areas gave him the yips when he was on a job, but he needed a toilet…*right now*. He should never have had that second cup of coffee, he thought. Four miles later he saw an exit marked as having a rest stop. A little unusual, he thought. Rest areas were usually right off the highway. Didn't matter. Scorp guided the Suburban off the exit ramp. He turned left at the stop sign. Entering a four lane divided highway he noticed there were county work vehicles parked on the shoulder. And a little further up there were logging trailers with huge stripped pines filling their jaws. He saw a *Rest stop ahead* sign. Relief in sight. The shoulder of the highway dropped off sharply. He could see where those giant pines on the logging trucks came from. They'd been cut down along the stretch of road, and it looked like the county was adding an exit to tie into the rest area.

Scorp checked his phone. When he looked up, he realized a car making a right hand turn in front of him had come to a stop.

6

Reasons

"**Y**ou want another coffee, Jo? I'm havin' one. Let's go out on the deck." They'd spent fifteen minutes searching for any sign of Erik. They were satisfied Erik was gone.

"Sure, Candy. Another coffee would be great. Thanks."

"It's a little chilly. Here's a jacket." Candy tossed Jo a windbreaker and Jo whisked her scarf back and put the jacket on. They went out on the deck off Candy's second floor bedroom suite. There was a slight breeze and the sun was bright, but not reaching the deck area yet. They sat down on the cushioned wicker chairs.

"So, Jo, how did you sleep last night? I thought about waking you up and finding a bed for you, but I didn't want to disturb either of you guys. Was the couch OK?"

"Oh, well, honestly, my neck is killing me. I'm so sorry, Candy. Look, I know what I did last night and it wasn't right. I apologize. I led you to think, well, you know. There's no excuse. I'd like to try to explain if you'd let me?" Jo took a long sip of her coffee and set her mug down on the side table.

"Well, Jo, I have to say, I was a little disappointed. I'm not attracted to most women. Maybe one in a thousand. If you aren't interested in me that way, it's all good. I could use a plain old friend right now. NSA friends is cool if we click. Maybe we could go shopping, get some food, whatever. See if we wanna' hang out more? You don't owe me an explanation, Jo. If you changed your mind, it's OK." Candy had struggled with her own bisexuality for years. She wondered if her father had something to do with it? Maybe she felt conflicted giving all her love to a man? By the time she was eighteen, she no longer wished to hide her desires. She was who she was.

Jo was studying Candy. She'd taken in every word and analyzed it. Candy's body language. Her words. The tone she was using. She'd decided Candy was being a hundred percent honest.

"I'm truly sorry, Candy. I wouldn't have done that in the club bathroom if I wasn't interested. That isn't something I do on the regular. In fact, I've never done that before. Not sure why I did, but now…well, I'm glad I did. It's just…when I saw this place I freaked. I was thrown off. I mean, we aren't from the same side of the tracks. I felt, like, completely out of place. Intimidated. And Erik? He's very, very odd. I should've left last night, and thought I would, but then Erik was so freakin' weird I didn't want to leave with him here, with you. It all just weighed on me, so I took a pill, fell asleep, and then…well you know the rest.

"Oh, Jo…geez. I understand. Wow. I've been in that situation before. Not fittin' in I mean. Not cool. Yeah, and Erik is weird. I'll give you that. The boy is one of those fuckin' gen Z'ers. I could've slapped that phone out of his hands. I'm glad he left. His loss."

"Me too, Candy…me too. Glad he left. He's a creeper. I caught him looking at you in the van. Thought he was going to dive into your shirt. He had this weird look on his face. He seemed so harmless at the club."

"And, Jo, so you know, this isn't my house. I'm just visiting. I've lived in cars, crack houses, nasty trailer parks and cheap motels my entire life. So, I understand why you reacted the way you did. Just try to enjoy this place. That's what I'm doing." Candy wasn't happy she had lied to Jo. Jo deserved the truth. She would tell her the truth when the time was right. For now, she thought it best to hide her ownership of the house since Jo was so overwhelmed.

"Ok, Candy, I'll try. And again, I'm sorry about last night. Let's just go slow, OK?"

"Sure. No problem. How about this. You wanna go shopping with me today, Jo? Grab some food and try some stuff on? Maybe you know some good places to shop? All I do is Amazon Prime. It's getting old. I order stuff online, try it on, return it. Over an' over.

I need to do real shoppin'. You can't touch clothes on the internet. And the colors aren't right."

"I wish I could, Candy. I've got an Uber coming in a few minutes. My brother is flying in and I have to pick him up at the Airport."

"Another time, Jo?"

"I'd like that. Just me and you. A fresh start, without Erik."

Candy watched from the bedroom deck. The Uber had pulled up and turned around. She watched Jo walk over to it and open the back door. Jo looked up, waved and got in. Gone. Back to being alone, Candy thought. Maybe she should volunteer at the animal shelter she'd seen in town. Join the Y and take a yoga class. Teach martial arts to kids. Meet people, make friends somewhere other than a bar, nightclub, or strip joint.

Candy couldn't help but wonder. Jo seemed so nervous this morning. Her hands were shaking. Kept adjusting her scarf. Maybe she was hungry? Why did she leave so abruptly? Candy didn't believe the "brother at the airport" excuse. She looked out at the fall sky. Beautiful day. Nice day…nice cars come out, she thought. Her Challenger needed to be exercised. And she needed to clear her mind and think about her new straight life. She was ready for normal.

She dressed, then grabbed her fob and purse, took the elevator to the garage level, and skipped over to her purple Challenger SRT8. She pushed the start button and took a deep breath, savoring the aroma of the rich leather interior.

Candy took the highway heading west, away from town. She lit a Newport and set the cruise. A few miles out she noticed a sign, up high on a crane that read *Essential Sales & Rental*. There were at least two dozen bucket trucks crowding the high chain link fence that lined the property, their buckets saluting the sky. And a row of giant tired CAT loaders. She'd ask Jim if that was his business. It was a huge equipment yard, covering a minute or more of high speed highway before disappearing from her rearview mirror.

7

No Texting, No Hand Held Phones

The car in front of him was stopped… dead. He was going too fast. Scorp swerved wildly to the right. The Suburban fishtailed, skidded on the narrow gravel shoulder, and left the road. The slope was severe, straight down. The Suburban's brakes were locked as it encountered the first tree stump. The SUV hit it quarter front, careened, picking up more speed as it headed further down the hill. It smashed into a clump of smaller stumps. Airborne. Tumbling. All fifteen airbags deployed. The full five-gallon emergency gas can that Scorp always carried, just in case, ignited, creating a fireball that consumed the interior. The Suburban's twenty-eight gallon gas tank ruptured. On his back, disoriented, Scorp tried desperately to open the door. The door creaked open, and he flung himself to the ground. Flames and toxic smoke rose up from the carcass of the Suburban. Scorp instinctively reached for his phone pocket. His hand stuck to the molten fabric. He couldn't see out of one eye, or feel his face. Twelve minutes passed before the first help arrived. A hook and ladder, followed by three highway patrol vehicles and an ambulance. They radioed for more help. A wrecker and a four wheel drive vehicle for the paramedics. The ambulance couldn't attempt a trip down that slope.

Scorp's Suburban was scorched down to bare metal. A wisp of smoke was curling around the last combustibles. Debris littered the hillside. The paramedics had scrambled down and examined Scorp. He had severe facial, neck, shoulder, and upper arm burns. Unconscious. Breathing was shallow. Shock symptoms. The four wheel drive rescue vehicle made its way down into the ravine and Scorp was transported to the closest hospital, Holy Savior Central Hospital.

The police were unable to find a witness to the accident. The occupant who'd been burned? No identification. He was a white male in his thirties. They'd have to speak with him when, or if, he regained consciousness. He wasn't going to be chatting with them anytime soon. They ordered a rollback and a crane with a dolly to remove the Suburban. No rush. It wasn't going anywhere. And the only place the poor bastard who'd been driving it was going was the ER.

8

Trailer Trashed

Candy just drove. Back roads. Windows down, sunroof open, Alpine stereo cranked. She exited the highway to test a few back roads. Twisty and hilly. The roadside was dotted with shacks masquerading as houses. Chickens scattering off to the shoulder now and then. Side and backyards landscaped with decades of rusted former transportation. Rotting porches trying to support moldy sofas. She drove for miles and noticed a small store. Some cigarettes and restroom, she thought.

Candy parked, stepped out and stretched. The grimy cinder block building boasted cigarette, videos, lottery, notary, and postage stamp signs stuck haphazardly to the filthy windows. One-stop shop in Nowhereville, she thought. Candy opened the dented aluminum door and went in. She bought her Newports from the tooth free ancient woman behind the counter. At least they had her brand. Probably stale, she thought.

"Got a restroom?"

"Round back, honey. No key. My son might be using it right now, so be sure to knock." The old woman eyed Candy up and down, slowly, and grinned. Candy felt the hair on her arms stand up in reaction.

"Thanks. I'll be sure to knock."

Candy walked out and around. She'd decided on a quick stop and then she was getting back on the main highway and making her way back to her house. The twisty roads and depressing scenery were tiring. And not the scenic drive she'd hoped for. But it had given her time to think. She'd try to become friends with Jo, wait for Scorp to come home, and sell the drugs as she had promised. Time to grow up and deal with life as a functioning adult. A life without chemical support. She remembered one of her clients suggesting she might want to see a therapist. She'd experienced a meltdown during a "session," tossed him off the bed, pinned him down, threatened him, dragged him outside, and threw him down the stairwell at her motel. Couldn't hurt to talk to someone, she thought. Discuss her anger issues, drug use and how to deal with the recurring nightmares of the sexual and emotional abuse she'd suffered at the hands of her father.

She knocked on the bathroom door and opened the crusty, rusty bathroom door. He pushed her, *hard*. Candy stumbled backwards, falling to the graveled ground. She tried to break her fall. Her head hit a concrete block. Woozy, she got to her knees, wobbled, and stood up.

"What the fuck, asshole. Who the fuck you think…," she screamed. He was tall. Sickly thin. Big black results of what started as pick marks the size of walnuts on his cheeks and forehead. Oscillating eyes. Body odor stench. Just a few rotted teeth protruding from black gums. Candy knew. Meth head. Tweaker. The smoke following him out of the bathroom confirmed her diagnosis. This would be so easy, she thought. He'd picked the wrong girl. If she could shake the dizziness….

"Hey, baby! Wanna wanna party with me? Got plenty a glass for both of us. My trailer's in them woods back there." He pointed with both arms to a path that dropped off through the woods behind the store. He stumbled forward, reached, and found Candy's breast, then squeezed, *hard*.

"Nice boobies girl. Owwwhoo!…Let's share them with my little brother, yeah yeah? Come on."

Candy winced in pain and locked onto his arm. She felt faint and had to relax her grip. The tweaker groaned, encircled her waist, twirled and slammed her head against a cast iron drainage pipe, knocking her out. He picked her up and threw her over his shoulder, then headed down a well-worn trail into the dense woods behind the store, to the dilapidated, decades old trailer he called home.

9

Savior So Holy

Scorp was rushed to the ER. His clothes were cut off and IVs started. Fluids and antibiotics. He had third degree burns on his face and second degree on his arms. His torso and lower limbs has escaped damage. Less than twenty percent total body area had been burned. In an hour he regained consciousness.

"Can't feel my face. Where am I?"

The young nurse told him where he was and left, returning with the attending physician.

"You were in a bad accident. We will need to get some information from you. You're going to be OK. I know you are in pain. We'll start a drip." His doctor leaned forward to get a better look.

"My arms…fuck!"

"Your arm burns will be painful. I'm sorry. You won't have any facial pain… yet. We're going to make sure the areas don't get infected. Your nurse will be changing your dressings frequently."

The doctor ordered an antibiotic cream for his arms. "You are going to be here about a month, possibly longer. We'll have to see how you progress. You'll need skin grafts for your facial burns. We'll discuss that in a week or so."

"I need to leave soon, Doc. I can't be here a month. That won't work."

"You need to heal properly. And there's a risk of infection." The doctor ordered a strong sedative, and told the nurse to show him his face during her next shift. That was a tactic he had used before to convince a patient to follow directions.

Holy Savior didn't have a designated burn unit. Scorp's injuries didn't appear to be life threatening, so the staff decided he wouldn't need to be transferred to another facility.

The following day, the nurse and a social worker visited Scorp. He was uncooperative. Refused to answer questions regarding himself, insurance, or next of kin. The social worker explained that in cases like his, with no information to work with, he would be released as soon as the threat of infection was over. His doctor would make that decision. Later in the day, the local police department sent an officer to interview him. Same result. No answers offered up. The crash victim would not cooperate. They had not been able to locate a VIN number on the Suburban and the license plates were not in good enough condition to decipher. The officer asked a few more questions, made notes, and left. The burn victim had little memory of the accident.

"I'm OK. Don't need anything." His nurse had asked if he needed something for the pain. He needed to be clearheaded. "Is my cell here?"

Scorp's phone held the vault code. The code he changed before he left to ensure Candy wouldn't use the drugs. The vault was purchased through a third party and he had that information in his missing phone too. "Fucking technology," he cursed under his breath. He hadn't backed up any information to the Cloud. Didn't trust the Cloud, for security reasons. What the hell was it, anyway? How could he pay Abe and Jamey without access to the vault? The four hundred seventy-five thousand he owed them went up in smoke. They wanted their cash and they'd be coming for it. He didn't know Candy's cell number. He didn't know anybody's number. Who kept numbers in their head these days? He couldn't even remember his home address.

"No sir. No cell phone, or identification. Nothing. You came in with nothing. From what I heard, your vehicle and everything in your vehicle, was destroyed in the fire." His nurse answered his questions as well as she could. She was in her late twenties. A little chubby but pretty and proportioned. She felt bad for her latest patient, even though he was being uncooperative. When she'd showed him his facial burns, he didn't react. That was unusual.

The right side of his face and neck would be horribly scarred if he didn't follow orders correctly and follow through with proper skin graft procedures. And refusing painkillers? All burn victims needed meds. Maybe not the first or second day, but by day three the pain would start to be felt in areas previously numb. His face would remain pain free. The skin there was red and leathery. She'd make sure it stayed dressed properly. His arms would be extremely painful as the burns were less severe. This man was tough. She wondered who he was and where he came from. And she couldn't help but notice what a physical specimen he was while attending to him. She'd never seen a man…like him.

10

Three's A Crowd

Candy opened her eyes. She could taste blood. It was running down her face from surface lacerations she'd suffered from being slammed into the drainage pipe outside of the bathroom. Her wrists were bound. Something was propping her midsection up, and she couldn't move her legs. The aroma of cat piss was overwhelming. The signature cologne of a meth house, she thought. And whiffs of what she thought smelled like a hospital ward mixing in confirmed her suspicions. She decided to be still. Quiet. Wait. She could hear the background sound to what had to be a porn movie, and two male voices appeared to be close by.

"Spank her hard, Dave. That'll wake her up. I want her awake for this." The older brother Sam was directing. Candy could see a cloud of smoke and smelled a light, sweet odor. Then she felt the first slap. She let out a breath, sucked in, and waited for the next. It landed. Harder this time.

"Hey, guys, let me loose. Let's party. I'm your girl. I'll do whatever you want if you cut me free."

"Told you that would wake her up… I'm, I'm, I'ma goin' first, Dave. I found her. You play with her tits an' I'll take care of the rest."

Candy wasn't an expert on meth heads. Methamphetamine wasn't popular in Jersey or Maryland. It was a rural drug. Meth production labs needed to be hidden well, away from prying eyes. She'd heard stories of meth marathon sex orgies and that many males high on meth thought they were "Kings" and that women wanted them, no matter how disgusting they looked or smelled. Part of the drug's enhancement. Unsubstantiated confidence. She'd try to tap into that drug induced skewed mentality for an advantage. Her head was pounding.

Candy felt rough hands on her breasts, but couldn't move, or see. She was spanked over and over until she couldn't feel it anymore. Then, she felt, a finger? Then, something much wider and longer.

"Hey guys, feels good! Cut me loose and I'll take it somewhere else." She had to convince them they would have more fun if they untied her. No answer. What seemed like an hour passed by. Long nails were digging into her hips and rear. Her breasts were nearly numb from the little brother squeezing and tugging. She heard a grunt, then saw smoke.

"Your turn, Dave. Stick her in the other hole."

"Guys…Cool! I love anal! Let me free and we can double penetrate. I want both of you at the same time…come on! You two are fuckin' awesome. You got nice ones. I want more!" No answer. Her idea of complimenting her captors wasn't working. She took a deep breath as he put it in.

Another, what seemed to be an hour. Another cloud of smoke. They were using something else on her now. Together. How long could this go on? She felt liquid running everywhere. Bleeding below? She felt faint and passed out. When she came to she could hear sex sounds. But no one was touching her.

"That's it, Dave, just like that…yeah…don't stop now…now… now…."

Candy could hear it, clearly. The two men were tired of her and enjoying each other now. She could hear thrusting and slapping mixed in with sensual moans and groans.

"Hey, guys, are you done with me now? Let me go." No answer. Her head was throbbing and her arms and legs were numb. There was searing pain below. If they used her again she thought she would die…right there. Die face down on a smelly, bloody mattress. In a trailer, in Nowhereville. She scolded herself. She should have stayed home. Safe. Secure. And now this. If Scorp had just stayed home with her, none of this would have happened. Her cell was in her car, in the console. Her backpack was in the car too. She needed to get free. Get to her car.

"Hey guys! I got a lotta money at my house. Enough to keep ya' in crystal for a month. But you gotta cut me free. Untie me an' I'll take you to my house. I can get another girl to join us too." If she could get her hands free she could escape. She could overwhelm them with her skills. No chance tied up and face down. It was so frustrating not being able to move, or see what they were doing. Not knowing what would be next in store for her. Frustrating, and frightening. They might just wander off and forget she was even there. Move on to another unfinished project.

No answer.

"What the hell are you boys doing?" Candy recognized the voice. The smoky voice of the old woman storekeeper. Her sons were naked and playing on the couch.

"You know the Lord don't approve of men being with men. Now stop it! Right now!"

"K, Mom." They sprang up off the couch, and put their pants on quickly. Sam spoke up. "Mom, we're real sorry. Just got a little carried away."

"OK, son. Don't like it, but I understand how the Tina works on ya'. Let's share some glass." The sons and their mom filed up their glass bowls. Candy could hear their powerful butane lighters hiss and then saw smoke swirling in front of her.

"Now, you boys pull them pants back down. The Lord says Mamas should take care of their babies."

Candy thought out loud in a whisper. "Fuck, I've been captured by a multi-generation freaky tweaker family. And all I wanted was a nice ride in the country." She hummed to avoid hearing the family perversions taking place somewhere behind her.

11

True Lies

Jo liked her. Candy wasn't like any other woman she'd met. She thought Candy would be fun to be around. She even enjoyed Candy's Jersey accent and attitude. Jo hated lying to Candy. Hated lying in general. The "brother at the airport" story so she could get away and think wasn't something she was proud of. Jo decided she had to tell Candy what *really* happened last night. She was ready to talk now.

Jo was finishing her early morning shift at the diner. The tips had been good. She'd been working there for a few months. She'd had a decent, salaried job at Essential Sales & Rental, but she'd resigned due to the workplace conditions. Jo was sad she had to quit. She loved the job, and the owner, Jim Griot, couldn't have been nicer. But the office manager was evil. The rumor was she had a revolving bedroom door. She discriminated against Jo her first day on the job. All the employees who worked under the supervision of Laura Morningstar were allowed to keep a flexible work schedule, except Jo. Jo was told she needed to ask when she needed to use the restroom, or take her lunch break. She was also the only staff member who wasn't allowed to park out front of the building. Laura insisted Jo park where the company mechanics parked their trucks. Every morning when she got out of her tiny sports car, some of the guys would jeer and whistle at her. It was humiliating. Jo was highly valued for her inventory management skills by the owner. He also sought her help on special company projects. Jim Griot had planned on making her the office manager and demoting Laura. A few of the other office employees harassed her also, making it difficult to do her job. It had become unbearable. Her intent was to sue. But that wasn't on her mind now. She needed to call Candy. She punched out, got in her Miata, and tapped on Candy's number. No answer. She texted. No answer. She went home and tried again. No answer. She shivered. They *had* to talk. *Soon.* She decided to drive to Candy's house, tell her everything, and try to clean up the mess she was in. It wouldn't be easy, she thought.

By the time she made it to Candy's place, it was early evening. The driveway and landscaping were defined by strategic lighting. There were lights on inside. Good. Candy was home, she thought. Then, she saw them. Outside of the gated entrance, there were two state police cars. They were parked side by side, and the officers were talking through the windows, gesturing, holding up their phones. Jo drove past, down the steep hill, and stopped to think. What were they doing at Candy's house?

Jo tried Candy's cell again when she got home. No answer. Where could Candy be? Why wasn't she answering? Could she have found...? Was that why the cops were there?

12

Telltale Tag

Abe and Jamey were stymied. They'd tried calling Scorp's cell all night. No answer. They didn't know Scorp's full name or have his address. There was no time for sleep. Every minute that passed could mean he was further away from them, spending *their* paycheck.

Abe had an idea. "Check your phone pics, Jamey. Didn't you get his license plate during that job a few months back?"

"Maybe. I think I remember taking a pic the only time I had a chance to, but let me see."

He scrolled through the gallery on his Android. There were hundreds of pics of cars, SUV's and trucks. Jamey was a vehicle freak.

"This could be it, Abe. Don't know why I would've taken this except to get the tag." The picture was of a large black SUV that appeared to be a Chevy Suburban. Just the tailgate, bumper and tag number were featured. It was a bit blurry, but the tag was readable. The date stamp was two years old.

"OK, Jamey. We gotta do something. Let's see where that tag leads us. Beats sitting here. Any other pics like this you see?"

"Well, there's a few, but I'm pretty sure this is Scorp's. It was the only time I ever saw what he was driving, so I took it real quick… snuck it. Back then we didn't trust him much. Should have known he'd fuck us over. Low life SOB. How we gonna work it, Abe?"

"I know a cop. It'll cost us ten grand. Running tags for somebody could cost him his job and pension. Gotta make it worth his while."

"Guess there ain't no warranty if it turns out it ain't his tag. It's either Scorp's tag or we are screwed out of ten grand."

"Spending ten to get our 400…we gotta do it." Abe got up. "I'll be back. Text me that tag pic. Stay here in town somewhere and I'll pick you up when I'm done. Might take a few days."

Abe made the call, did the drive, and paid the fee to his LE connection, who had transferred to a different location. The tag was registered to Candise Doubleday, with a New Jersey address. Abe had initially checked the New Jersey and Maryland judicial case search records. He thought they might get lucky—save money and a drive. No record for Candise Doubleday. Not even a speeding ticket. But now, they had a name and address. A good start. He called Jamey with the news. "Road trip time, partner. We're headed to Jersey. I'll pick you up."

Abe and Jamey pulled up to the address they were given. "I thought it would be a house. This looks like some sort of warehouse." Abe stopped at the locked gate.

"I don't know, Abe. Beats me. Let's check it out." There was a For Sale sign zip tied to the dilapidated entrance gate. The entire property was surrounded by an eight-foot-high chain link fence topped with razor wire.

They parked across the street and walked around to the rear side of the property, away from the street. Abe used bolt cutters on the fence and they were in. Breaking a window, they entered the main building. The first floor was completely empty. As if no one had ever stepped foot inside. They made their way upstairs. It looked like a normal rancher, with bedrooms, a kitchen, and several bathrooms. It was empty, like the first floor. No sign that anyone had ever lived there.

"OK, Jamey, we'll have to try something else." They took the back stairway down. Abe noticed a small trash bag under the staircase as they were about to leave. "Let's have a look at the trash and we'll check the trashcans outside too."

Abe dumped the trash bag and started sifting through it. Empty Newport 100 boxes, cigarette butts, McDonalds bags, an empty baggie, used condoms, and some crumpled papers. He unraveled the papers. One was a real estate ad. A half-page ad for a house in Annapolis, Maryland. The ad was circled and had stars drawn in across the top. "Here we go, Jamey." He called the realtor listed in the ad and read the MLS number to him. That house had been sold quite some time ago.

"I'm looking for a house similar to the one in your ad and in that same area. Could you give me the address of this one so my wife and I could do a ride by? Abe thanked him and googled the address. "We'll check this house out, Jamey. *Somebody* thought it was special. Maybe it'll lead us to Scorp. We got nothing else to work with."

They stopped at Men's Wearhouse and bought some business suits, shirts, ties, and wingtips, then drove to Annapolis. They located the upscale cul-de-sac development easily, parked, and approached the house that had been circled in the ad and rang the doorbell.

"Can I help you?" A middle-aged man answered the door. He had cracked the storm door just enough so they could hear him.

"Yes, sir. Maybe you can help. We're finalizing a claim for the Buffalo Insurance Company and are trying to locate Ms. Candise Doubleday. This is the last address we had for her. By chance is she here? We have a settlement check for her."

"No, she doesn't live here. I don't know that person. We're renting through an agency."

"Would there be anyone else in the neighborhood who might know how we could locate Ms. Doubleday?"

"I can't help you." He slammed the front door.

"Jamey, let's knock on *all* these doors. Someone might know her."

"OK, Abe. Have a feeling we are going to be treated like Seventh Day Adventist fuckers."

They started down the sidewalk and noticed a young woman with a toddler in hand across the street. "Let's talk to her, Jamey." They crossed over and approached the attractive pregnant woman.

"Good evening, Miss. We are with the Buffalo Insurance Company and we're trying to locate Candise Doubleday. We have a settlement check for her. We understand she may have lived in that house." Abe pointed to the house they'd just left.

"Well yes, I do know her. She is, er…was a good friend. Haven't seen her since she moved out. She's in Tennessee, I think. I'm not sure. It's been some time."

"Would you have a cell number for Ms. Doubleday. I'm sure she'd like to receive this check."

"Nah, don't have that. Wish I did. I'd love to talk to her. If you find her, would you give her my number, and ask her to call me? Or text me her number? Please? My name's Gina. I really, really need to talk to her."

"Certainly, Miss Gina." Jamey put her number into his contacts. Here, take my business card. Jamey handed her the bogus business card he always carried. "Call us if you remember anything else that could help us locate Ms. Doubleday, OK? By the way, that's a pretty little girl you have there. What's her name?"

"Lily. And she'll have a little sister soon." Gina patted her baby bump.

"Well, congratulations! And thanks again." Abe and Jamey got in the new Jaguar F Pace SUV and looked at each other. "Man, Abe, that's the hottest pregnant woman I've ever seen."

"Yeah, Jamey, she's hot. You did see the size of her stomach and the little kid though, right? Let's head to Tennessee. Just a matter of time now, Jamey."

13

Home Not So Sweet

Gina let herself in, gave Lily a bath and put her to bed, then joined Audrey and Syd in the family room. She had moved in with the married couple after Candy and Scorp moved out of the house they had been renting across the street. Candy said she and Scorp were building a house in Tennessee, and David Haspert, the dentist who lived with the three of them briefly, was moving to a condo. Gina had nowhere to go. She couldn't go back to sex work. She despised it. Only being with Candy had made it bearable. So she'd given in and moved in with the odd couple. It seemed safe and was free. Or so she thought.

"You should have had a jacket on, Gina. It's chilly out there. Don't want you to catch a cold sweetie." Gina was so weary of Audrey mothering her. She treated her like she was fifteen.

"Yeah, I know. I'll remember next time."

"Who were those men you were talking to?" Audrey was the neighborhood snoop. Nothing escaped her.

"Oh, they're looking for Candy. Insurance guys. They have a check for her."

"I see. You haven't heard from her, have you?" Audrey was glad Candy and all those other scary people moved out. She and her husband Syd took Gina and Lily in when the others moved. Such a strange group those old neighbors were, Audrey thought. She didn't think Gina could care for the little girl properly, so she'd convinced Syd having her stay with them awhile would be the right thing to do. Audrey knew Gina was close to being evicted from the rental house. She and her daughter would be homeless.

Syd couldn't hide his attraction to the gorgeous, quiet young woman living with them. Gina had agreed to be intimate with Syd and Audrey as part of their housing offer. Audrey couldn't explain her newfound bisexuality, how or why it became part of who she now was. The encounter she had with Gina at a pool party hosted by Candy last year, at the house across the street, had confirmed that she enjoyed women as much as men. She had always been open with Syd. He was not one to judge. And she wasn't jealous of Gina. She was attracted to her as much as Syd, maybe more. Within a few months, Syd was successful. Gina was pregnant, with a girl. Audrey had been praying that would happen. She was ecstatic. They would soon have the baby she had longed for, and was unable to have.

Syd patted the sofa, and Gina sat between them. He kissed her on the cheek and patted her bump. "Won't be long now we'll have more women in the house. Not bad for an old man, huh?"

Gina reached out and held hands with them. "Not bad at all, Syd, not bad."

14

Travel Nurse

"**W**hat's your name?" He needed a way to get home. Scorp's nurse was a possibility. Maybe he could convince her to help him. Knowing her name was a start.

"Khloe. Guess you won't tell me your name, huh?" She was giving him a sponge bath. Her thoughts meandered. She remembered the last burn victim she treated. He was wheelchair bound and caught himself on fire. He'd been smoking crack and used the kitchen stove to fire up a rock. He'd been burnt beyond recognition. It was three days before his regular hooker and dealer found him and managed to get him to the hospital. Khloe kept in touch with him briefly after he'd been discharged. He'd been accepted into a rehab program.

"Name's Scorp. Like in Scorpion without the ending. We even now?"

"Fair enough, Scorp." She lifted his arm and he winced. "Hurts like hell doesn't it? I can give you something for the pain. It's going to be with you awhile."

"What I really need, Khloe, is to get back home. Tennessee. At least I remember what state I'm from. I'll have to figure out where exactly. I remember the house is at the top of some mountain. You're very cute by the way. Glad you aren't one of them other nurses I've seen around here. About the only luck I've had lately is landing you."

Khloe smiled. He was nice. The side of his face was a mess. His neck was in bad shape too. His shoulders and upper arms hadn't escaped the flames either.

"You know when they'll release me, Khloe?"

"Tomorrow, if your doc thinks the chance of you getting an

infection has passed." Four days had passed since Scorp had been admitted to Holy Savior.

"All my clothes, money, phone, everything is gone. I sure could use some help getting home. Could we talk about that?"

"Help from who? Me?"

"Khloe, I wouldn't ask but I'm in bad shape and all my money is at my house. Don't use credit cards or nothing like that. Look, I'm not expecting you to help me for nothing. I have lots of money I made in the car business. I'm retired now. I'll give you five years pay in cash if you help me get home. Please, think about that. I'm in a real bad situation. You help me and I'll help you. What do you think?"

"I have to make my rounds, Scorp. Let me think. You know, I don't even know you."

Later in the day, after punching out, Khloe went to Scorp's room.

"Five years pay is about three hundred fifty thousand, Scorp. I'll help get you home for four hundred thousand. I don't know you. Don't even know your *real* name or what kind of person you are. I'd be taking a big risk. Four hundred thousand. Could pay off my mortgage and help my mom out." She tried not to show any emotion. Offers like his were only found in dreams. She studied him. He seemed to be sincere. And she had no doubt he needed help. He appeared to have a mild case of trauma amnesia. That might clear up spontaneously. It was now or never. She'd been so conservative and careful her entire twenty-eight years. His proposition was exciting in a scary kind of way.

"That's cool, Khloe. Four hundred. It's a deal. Might take a week or more to get there...not sure." No house keys. No vault combination. And his associates were surely looking for him. If he could get through this, he'd made up his mind. Retire, propose to Candy and start a family. A real, crime-free family. Maybe even finance a shelter for abused women, or a rehab center. Candy would love that.

Khloe had decided quickly. She feared he might offer the money to someone else. "I can take some emergency leave. We can leave tomorrow morning. I'll get you some clothes tonight. No one here at the hospital can find out about this." Khloe wasn't married, had no children and no boyfriend. Not even a dog, cat, bird, or fish. Leaving on short notice wasn't a problem. And the money made it a risk worth taking. "Can I trust you, Scorp?" She moved closer and focused on his eyes.

"Yes, Khloe. You can trust me. Look, I'm helpless. I'm good for the money. I just have to get home. I'll give you the money and you can be on your way. I have a girlfriend who lives with me. It's nothin', you know, like that. It's just business between me and you."

"So, if you have a girlfriend, why don't you just call *her*? Get her to pick you up?"

"I don't have her number or I would. My phone had everything on it."

"So, get a new phone and transfer the data."

"It's not that simple. I'm careful about stuff. There isn't any call history or things like that. Her number was just a number in my notes. I know it sounds weird. It's just that I have money and I'm super careful about all my private information. There's always somebody who's tryin' to get your money one way or another. Look, I need a laptop to use too. I can't remember the house address, but we can find it online, I think. Look, I need to know I can trust you too. I can't just take a bus home. Please, help me."

"OK, Scorp. It's looking like you will be released in the morning. I'll put in for my leave. Once I have a discharge time I'll have an Uber pick you up here and bring you to my place and we can leave from there." She had an idea of sizes she'd buy for his clothes. "I'll have someone bring you clothes and shoes early tomorrow morning."

"Thank you, Khloe! I'm so glad I met you. You'll see, it'll all work out." He had a ride. A travel nurse. If he needed anything, she'd be able to help.

His clothes arrived early, as Khloe had promised. Around 8 a.m., his Doctor showed up and said he'd be released at ten. He was wheeled out at ten twenty and the Uber was waiting for him. At Khloe's, he got into her beat up green '98 Honda Accord sedan.

15

Detourlicious

She fingered his business card. Jamey Bellis, Buffalo Insurance Company, New York. Just two hours had passed since she'd talked with the two insurance agents who were looking for her beloved Candy. Gina verified that Syd and Audrey were sound asleep, went to her bedroom and made the call.

"Mr. Bellis? This is Gina Lamartina. We met earlier. You'd asked me about Candise Doubleday. Could we meet tomorrow? I'd like to talk to you about locating her. Would that be possible?"

"Why absolutely, Ms. Lamartina. When and where would you like to meet?" Jamey looked over and winked at Abe, putting his phone on speaker.

"Denny's. On West Street in Annapolis. Does eleven work?"

"Perfect. That works for us. Thanks, Miss Lamartina. See you soon."

"Yeah, see you then. And call me Gina."

"Turn around, Abe. We got ourselves a good looking detour."

16

Road Trip

Khloe helped him with his seatbelt. She'd brought a fleece blanket to cushion him a bit. And she had burn salve, thirty Oxycodone tablets, yards of dressing to cover his burns, and a cooler with water and snacks. "OK, Scorp, so where are we heading? I have ten days." She pulled out an old Garmin and attached it to the windshield with a suction cup holder.

"For now, set it for Nashville and give me an ETA, Khloe. An' good morning. Relax."

She entered *Nashville.* "It looks like it will take a couple, maybe three days. Does that sound right?"

"I guess. Not sure how far the house is from Nashville, Khloe. I wish I could help with driving, but I don't even have my license. An' thanks for the clothes. Nice soft big stuff. We can get a cheap motel room when we have to stop. Two rooms, I mean. Course I'll pay you back for all expenses. You bring a laptop?"

"Yes, sir. All set. Let's get going." Khloe lit a cigarette. She hadn't smoked in five years, but this called for chain smoking.

"Can I have one?" Scorp was pointing to her Marlboro.

"Sure…I'm a little surprised you smoke."

"Me too, Khloe…me too."

Scorp was deep in thought. The *old* Scorp would have just knocked Khloe out, taken her cash, credit cards, and car and tossed her in a ditch. He thought maybe *that* Scorp had faded away? The accident, his injuries and memory loss were weighing on him. And then the thought of Abe and Jamey coming after him was sobering. If they got to Candy first it wouldn't be good. He knew what Abe was capable of. A high probability Candy wouldn't survive it, even as tough as she was. He dozed off. When he woke up it was early evening. Time to look for a motel. Khloe'd been driving all day, only stopping for gas. And she hadn't slept at all last night.

"We just need a clean room, or rooms, and Wi-Fi, Khloe." Scorp was tired. Even after the long nap.

"OK, Scorp. The next exit with lodging, we'll stop". She'd decided it would be one room. It didn't make sense to let him out of her sight. Anything could happen. And he wasn't in good enough shape to try any funny business. She'd stay close to Scorp and make sure the agreement turned out as described.

They pulled into the motel entrance and Khloe parked and registered. They'd found a Bedtime Six with Wi-Fi. Khloe checked in and helped Scorp out of the car. She could almost feel the pain he was in. They made their way to their room and she ordered pizza. She could've used a stiff drink, but didn't want to let her guard down. She ordered a liter of Mountain Dew and some cinnamon sticks to go with the pizza.

"I'm using the bathroom." Khloe was uneasy about taking her clothes off around Scorp, even in a locked bathroom. She'd clean up quickly. Scorp just nodded. He was on her laptop and jotting down notes. He seemed distracted enough and she thought he'd be occupied for a while.

Scorp hadn't even looked up. He was googling furiously, trying to find a clue to his home address. It was taking his mind off the searing pain. Khloe picked out a change of clothes and her toiletries, went into the tiny bathroom, and locked the door. She turned on the water and jumped in. She hoped the noise would disguise her sobs. It'd finally got to her. She had to pull herself together.

17

Free To Flee

How long had she been tied up in this stinky, filthy place? Must have been at least six, eight hours? There wasn't any ambient light coming in. Maybe it was night?

Candy cried out. "Anybody here? Helloooo?" Nothing. Mom and the "boys" were either asleep or had left. Candy doubted they were asleep. She nodded off. When she woke up her scalp was itching horribly. Instinctively Candy reached. Her hand was free! Both hands free. And her ankles too. She tried to roll over off whatever was jammed under her and fell to the floor. She couldn't sit up. Then she noticed. Right in front of her. Flip-flops and bright pink toenails.

"Just try to stretch a bit and wait till you're ready before sitting up, honey. Prolly don't have no feelin' in your arms an' legs. I've been there. Just take your time. I'm gonna help you." Thick candied Southern accent. "Don't fret, hon. I'm the only one here. Nobody's gonna hurt you."

It took some time, but gradually Candy got feeling back in her arms and legs.

"Here, let me help you sit up. You're a mess. What's your name? Mine's Tracy Lynne."

"Candy. Is there any water here, Tracy Lynne? Bottled water?" She noticed stacks of coloring books and broken crayons everywhere. There was a dismantled engine on the kitchen table. Who was this woman helping her?

Tracy Lynne brought her a bottle of cold water and watched Candy try to sip. Her lip was cut and swollen. Some of the water was swallowed. The rest ran down her chest.

"Where did they go? I have to get outta here!" Candy tried to stand up. Tracy Lynne steadied her.

"Candy, babe, go slow. They really worked you over. But they won't be back for awhile. They cooked some meth up somewhere around here yesterday. They're off in the woods, I guess. It's OK. I just came over here to pick up some glass and found you all tied up. I'll help you. I'm sure that's your car I saw at the store, right? Nobody round here has anything like that."

"It's a Challenger."

"Yep, that's the one I seen."

Candy was getting some feeling back in her legs. "Could you help me get some clothes on?"

"I'll do more than that." Tracy Lynne brought a soaped up washcloth and helped Candy clean up. "I feel bad for you girl. I know what they did. They done the same to me before. Thing is, they think you *liked* it. They get high for days and have no idea what they're doing. I seen them two cut down trees for three days straight for no good reason. They didn't really mean to hurt you. They're just messed up."

"I need to get home. Maybe go to the hospital." Candy started toward the door.

"Whoaaa, girlfriend. You ain't got no clothes on yet. It's at least half a mile to your car. Let me help you." Tracy Lynne searched and found Candy's shorts and top. "I don't see your undies, but here, put your shorts on if you can. And yeah, get tested while you're at the hospital. I'm not sure how clean those two are."

Candy pulled her shorts on carefully. She couldn't button up. It was just too painful. Tracy Lynne helped her with her top." Here, take my flip-flops. I don't need them. Mostly go barefoot."

Candy felt around in her shorts and found the fob to her car.

Tracy Lynne yanked on some kitchen drawers and found what she had come for. She stuck a baggie of glass shards in her pocket and stuffed some twenties into the cookie jar on the counter. "Alright, Candy, we're all set. Let's get you to your car."

They made their way very slowly out of the trailer. Tracy Lynne helped Candy hike the narrow, uphill footpath that led to the store. It started raining. The trail turned to slick mud. Candy was struggling, holding on to Tracy Lynne to for support and balance. She couldn't remember a time in her life when she was more miserable, except possibly when her father assaulted her the first time. The rain picked up. It was pouring now. Candy slipped, held on, and they both went down hard. Covered with mud, sticks, and leaves, Tracy Lynne got to her feet by rolling off the trail into the soggy grass for traction, then helped Candy right herself. "Well, now we look like twins, Candy." The joke was lost on Candy. She was exhausted. It took another half hour to make the trip. They walked across the littered back lot and made their way around to the front of the store. The rain stopped.

"Surprised your car is still here. Folks probably thought somebody important owned it and let it be. Didn't even take them fancy wheels!"

Candy managed her way into the Challenger. She opened her backpack and handed Tracy Lynne three hundred-dollar bills. "Here, this is for helping me." She pulled out her phone. "Gimme your number, Tracy." She put Tracy in her contacts, then took a picture of her and the store. "I don't smoke meth, but I do other stuff, so maybe we could get together sometime, Tracy. Tracy Lynne's too much to say. Can I just call you TL?" Candy wanted documentation that showed where she was and who she was with. The phone number and pictures were a start. She'd discuss it with Scorp when he got back. File a police report if he agreed. She was embarrassed that she had been overpowered and outsmarted.

Tracy Lynne had smoked a bowl while Candy was situating herself in the Challenger's bucket seat. She leaned in the window. Her muddy face nearly touching Candy. Her pupils were dilated and her eyes were jittery. "Sure, TL's cool. Thanks for the cash. But I didn't help you to get paid, sweetheart. I'd love to hang out with you. I'm not a full time tweaker. I don't smoke the shit all the time. And you're a pretty thing, even with all that blood and mud on you." She turned and skipped away, around the corner of the store, disappearing from sight. Candy put the window up, locked the doors, and pressed the start button. Set the navigation for *home*. There was no way she was going to put her seatbelt on. That would be too painful. She pulled out on the road slowly, getting her bearings and slammed the accelerator to the floor. The traction control kicked in helping her stay straight on the damp macadam. She drove about a quarter mile and let off the gas. A single tear ran down her cheek. She flipped the visor down. She had cuts on her forehead, bruises, a swollen, split lip, and a loose tooth. She'd check her phone later.

18

Bath Time At Bedtime Six

Khloe wiped her tears and sniffled. She put on baggy sweat pants, a sports bra, and an oversized sweatshirt. Scorp would need to be bathed and his burns attended to. She drew a warm bath and mixed in some body wash.

"OK, your turn, Scorp. She helped him undress and get in the tiny motel tub. "I'll be right back." Khloe hurried to her phone and texted her mom. Gave her mom the name and address of the motel. Typed that she would be gone a few weeks or more. That she was driving to Nashville for a much needed vacation with a friend and not to worry. She felt relieved that someone knew where she was.

"OK, here we go, Scorp. This beats trying to clean you up in a hospital bed."

Khloe put more body wash in the tub and on the thin motel washcloth. "I'm sorry this washcloth is so rough, Scorp. May as well give us sandpaper to work with. I'll alternate with my hands." She washed his back, legs, feet and privates. They both tried to ignore his arousal. Khloe thought that was actually a good sign. A sign he was feeling a little better. His erection didn't concern her. She'd seen that with many patients. What did concern her was *her* body's reaction. She stood up. "I'll get a towel." She pulled the tub stopper. "Just relax a minute. Then I'll dry you off and get your face dressing changed." He would need to keep his facial burns covered. She would make sure she kept the dressing clean and dry.

"Humph," Scorp grunted.

Khloe sat down on the bed and tried to breathe. Her face was hot. Flushed. And her body was getting ready in other ways too. She didn't want Scorp to see her until the feelings went away. She was surprised, and not surprised. What was left of him was hard to ignore. His muscle structure was magnificent. And she hadn't been with a man since her first year of college. She went back into the bathroom, helped him get up, and dried him off carefully. "There you go, Scorp. I'll shave you in the morning. Ready for a painkiller?"

"Yeah, I need something. Whatever you got."

Khloe gave him a thirty-mg. oxycodone pill. He wouldn't be getting an erection once that kicked in. She helped him into clean clothes.

"Care if I watch TV?" Khloe was under the covers. Her body was telling her to sleep, but her mind hadn't stopped racing. She was attracted to a disfigured mystery man who didn't talk.

"Sure, just no news. I hate news. Just hearin' it makes me crazy." Khloe put a reality show on. She didn't need a crazy Scorp.

In the morning, she checked out and they were back on the road, but needed to eat. "Bob Evans OK, Scorp?"

"Sure."

Scorp ordered a huge "big breakfast special." Khloe handed him another pill. "I know you're hungry, Scorp, but I have to tell you, Oxy sometimes causes serious constipation."

"Great, Khloe, that's all I need. Face messed up, popping painkillers, and now I won't be able to take a shi...." He stopped short. Khloe chuckled and smiled. He was *talking*.

They drove all day. Luckily, they were able to find another Bedtime Six with Wi-Fi. Khloe checked in. They repeated pizza. She'd bathe him later. Khloe didn't need to see Scorp naked. The last time was still on her mind. She'd show, or better yet, tell his girlfriend the correct way to wash him and treat his burns.

He was back on her laptop, eating pizza on the bed. "Got it, Khloe." Hours of research had paid off. He recognized the shell company name as soon as he read it. The company name he'd used to buy the house. Map quest driving directions were next. Nashville had been a good start. His house was about a few hours south of Nashville.

"That's great, Scorp. I bet you have a nice place, huh?"

"It's private and quiet, so if that's what you like, it's nice."

"I hope you have some soft washcloths." Khloe scrubbed her face, brushed her teeth, and got into bed. Out cold.

The next morning they drove in silence. Finally, Khloe spoke. "Looks like it rained hard here last night. Look at all the trees that fell down, Scorp."

"Yeah, must have been a heavy storm. We'll be there soon."

19

Enough

Gina'd had enough. Being eight months pregnant had its unique set of challenges, but worse than that was putting up with Syd and Audrey. Syd "visiting" every day, sometimes twice, along with Audrey now and then. Relentless sexual pursuit, no matter what time of month. Gina thought it was beyond an inconvenient annoyance, even with the fifteen hundred a month "allowance" they had agreed on. Gina thought Audrey might have *some* good intentions, but she was so controlling and opinionated it was impossible to tolerate her. Gina was done with the "arrangement." She'd only agreed to move in so Lily would have some stability, proper care, and normalcy. When Candy moved away with Scorp, it put Gina and Lily in a bind. Her choices were limited. Scorp made it clear Candy was his, and his alone. They didn't ask her to leave with them. She could try to get a job, return to a life of prostitution living in no tell motels with Lily, or accept Syd and Audrey's invitation. At the time the only decent choice she had was to move in with them. Audrey had explained that their offer was contingent on Gina having relations with Syd and her, anytime they wanted. She'd gone on to say this was to be a completely private affair. Gina could tell no one.

Pregnancy wasn't part of the plan. At least that part wasn't explained to her. Syd refused to wear protection. Audrey told her Syd was "shooting blanks" and that was the reason they didn't have children. Another reason they welcomed her and Lily. Lily represented the daughter they never had. It'd been great at first. They took Lily to the Washington Zoo, the National Aquarium, Port Discovery, Dutch Wonderland and bought her toys, books and clothes. Everything a little girl needed. Audrey helped Gina dye her hair and Gina returned the favor. Syd would like having two blondes on call, Audrey told her.

Audrey didn't work, so she was always home, except occasional shopping trips or lunches with girlfriends. Initially Gina was invited along, but after a few months she was left out. Gina figured that Audrey was concerned that her girlfriend's questions might somehow alert them to what was really going on. So, Gina was trapped in the house. Miserable and at their mercy.

Syd and Audrey bought Gina everything she needed. Her "allowance" wasn't needed for essentials, so she saved it. She had close to fifteen thousand. Syd and Audrey joked that she wasn't a very expensive surrogate mother. Gina wished she'd never met them. She regretted seducing Audrey when she, Candy, and Scorp had first moved into the neighborhood. She thought it might have been the cocaine she'd used that day. Good cocaine had an effect on her sexuality. It washed away her inhibitions That, she thought, could have caused her to pursue their "cute little neighbor." She remembered that every time she'd been in bed with Candy they were high, on something. She did love Candy, and if she was going to be intimate with a woman, it would be Candy, not Audrey. Gina'd been completely drug free since Candy and Scorp moved. She was sure she no longer wished to service Syd and Audrey whenever they felt the urge. What started out as warm and cozy was now uncomfortable and queasy. Syd treated her no better than the scores of men she'd serviced. He enjoyed jamming his cock down her throat balls deep until she gagged and couldn't breathe. She'd remembered Candy mentioning something about "near Nashville." It was a start, she thought. She'd take Lily and go to Nashville. Gina was positive Candy would welcome her. The fact that she was pregnant? Not so sure Candy would be thrilled. Lily had been an issue when they lived together. Candy was jealous of the time Gina spent with her daughter. Gina was praying Scorp would be OK with her moving in. She'd talk to him. Explain that drugs were so much a part of her former relationship with Candy. Explain that she was clean and sober now and would never touch Candy unless he approved. That she just wanted a normal life free of drugs. She would only stay with them long enough to find a job and then she'd leave. Make a home, a normal home, for her, Lily, and her new baby girl.

20

If It's Stiff, It Won't Fit

Candy pulled into the strip mall and parked between two cars. She looked at her wrists. They were bruised from being bound. Her nails were broken. She pulled out her phone. Jo had called a dozen times. No voicemail or texts from her, though. And she had a text from Jim.

Hi Candy. It's Jim. Care to join me at the club for a drink? I'll be there around seven tonight.

It was past 10 p.m. Candy wasn't sure how long she had been held captive. She texted Jim.

Hi, Jim. I'm so sorry. I haven't been feeling well. Raincheck?

Candy wasn't that far from home now. She'd call Jo when she got there. Fifteen minutes later she arrived. She opened the gates with her remote and pulled up to the front door. Using the car's door sill, she jacked her way out of the Challenger. She unlocked the front door, crawled up the stairs and into the bathroom. She adjusted the lever to a light, warm spray and slowly, carefully soaped up. Mud, leaf debris, blood and grass swirled their way to the drain. She was too sore to bend and reach her feet. A half hour later, she patted herself down carefully with a soft towel, rinsed her mouth, grabbed her phone, and slipped under the covers. Safe, but alone. She called Jo.

"Jo, hey it's Candy. I'm sorry I missed your calls. Been in a situation. What's up?"

"Oh, Candy, I'm so glad you called. I need to talk to you. Right now. Can I come over? I can be there in a half hour."

"OK, but I'm not feeling well. I'll open the gates. Park next to my car out front and come to the front door. Candy didn't want to be alone in the house tonight. She'd see if Jo could spend the night.

And whatever she needed to talk about seemed pretty important.

Candy met Jo at the front door. She'd tried to cover up some of her facial bruises with makeup but wasn't feeling confident about her looks. Her lip was split and swollen. That couldn't be hidden. Jo helped her upstairs to her bedroom.

"I have to lay down, Jo. Had a rough time, today, tonight? I guess both."

"What in God's name happened to you!" Jo was shocked. Candy had cuts and bruises as if she'd been beaten. And she could only see her face.

"It's not important. You wanted to talk?" Candy crawled into bed and propped her head up with pillows. She was under the covers with her robe on. Just her head, eyes, and forehead visible.

"It's about the other night. I…I…it's about Erik. I lied to you. He attacked me, Candy. In the garage. He woke me up and told me I had to see something and pressured me to take the elevator down to the floor below the garage. When we got down there he took me in a room off the hallway. Said he found a key to the door somewhere. The room was huge and full of computers, all wired together. Hundreds of them, he said. Erik said it was a mining operation, whatever that is. I told him I didn't feel comfortable sneaking around. He was all sweaty and rambling on about how lucky he was to find the two of us. It was so weird. He reached for me. I ran out and was in the elevator when he caught up to me. He forced his way in, pushed me aside, and the elevator stopped at the garage level. He dragged me out, threw me up against the wall, and started kissing me. His hands were all over me. I screamed and begged him to stop. He slapped me and started choking me. I couldn't breathe. I somehow got free and he chased me around the garage. He caught me again and I kneed him, then pushed him…hard. He fell backwards and hit his head on one of those pipe things you have coming out of the floor down there. He didn't move after that. I checked his pulse. He was dead, Candy…dead. I didn't know what to do. I should have told you, but I was *so* scared.

I just sat on the sofa and cried. Waited for you to wake up. I was going to tell you what happened right away. Then I thought you might think I did it on purpose…I don't know…I wasn't thinking right."

"So, he's still in the garage? Jesus, Jo…my God…he's dead in *my* garage?"

"Yeah. He's over on the other side, where you park your van. I don't know what to do. Should we call the police? I drove by once and there were cops sitting outside your gate. I thought maybe you found Erik and called them. Look at my neck. Jo pulled her signature scarf slightly aside. The side of her neck had bruises shaped like hands.

"No, of course I didn't find him. Those cops sit out there sometimes on break. And I don't know anything about a room full of computers. I need to go down and see."

"I really don't want to go down there, Candy. I…I…."

"I don't either, Jo. It's not a choice. Let's go."

"OK…OK…I'm going."

Candy was livid. How could this have happened? *All of this.* Being abducted and raped. Harboring a dead body in her garage. She slipped carefully into a pair of sweats and sneakers. "Lets go."

21

Framework

Jo was standing outside the elevator on the garage level. She was shaking and sobbing, her hands covering her face. She felt ill.

"Jo, there isn't time for crying. You can cry all you want later. We need to get him outta here, *now*. If my friend came home to this, he'd kill us both for being so stupid. Now let's see what we can do." Jo continued sobbing, facing away from the mess she'd made. Candy put her arm around her. "It's OK, Jo. Trust me. Pull yourself together. We can fix this, together. Everything will be just fine. I promise."

Erik's body was lying on its side, on the ground, on the far side of Candy's minivan. Candy saw a shoe sticking out as they approached.

Candy opened the van hatch. "Help me drag him around and put him in the van, Jo." She put the third row seat down flat and moved the second row forward.

"What? Where are we going? What are we doing? Shouldn't we call the police?"

"Don't worry about where we are going. I got this. We can't call the police. That won't work out good for us." Candy grabbed a foot. "Come on, Jo, help me." Candy knew calling the police wasn't an option. They'd never believe it had been an accident. Her criminal record was extensive and included aggravated assault charges along with a slew of others. What was on paper, in court documents, would count against her. Her father supposedly had her criminal records scrubbed. She wasn't sure. Candy feared a professional forensic detective would identify her and learn her past. She was a new person in this town with a violent past and a Jersey accent. No one would believe their story. Reporting Erik's death would set her and Scorp back, possibly forever. She couldn't let that happen. They were so close to their goal. She didn't come this far just to end up in jail.

Jo joined in and helped drag Erik's stiff, lifeless body around to the back of the van. They hoisted his legs in, then tried to lift his torso. Rigor was in full bloom. Erik's right arm was sticking out at an awkward angle, complicating the maneuver. "Get in and pull his legs, Jo. This ain't working."

Jo opened the sliding van door, crawled in and yanked on his leg but couldn't budge the body. "I can't move him, Candy. Help me." Candy went around the other side of the van and they each took a leg and pulled. Erik was almost in, but his extended arm was not even close. "Alright, we're gonna have to try something else, Jo."

Candy pulled the hatch down onto Erik's arm. It was sticking out a foot farther than the bumper. Candy surveyed the garage. She spied a tarp and some rope on a shelf. "I'll cover his arm up and we'll tie the hatch down. Grab that tarp and rope and that big wrench on the workbench."

"And then what?" Jo was shaking and sweating, tears running off her chin. "What then…huh? Where are we going?" Her hands were shaking. She dropped the wrench on Candy's foot.

"If you ask me that again, I'm droppin' him off at *your* house. Please, get in, calm down, and be quiet for a minute so I can think. I told you. It's all gonna be OK." Candy's day was now complete. Beaten, captured and gang raped by meth heads. Escaping and making it home, only to find out her new friend Jo hadn't told her there was a dead man in her garage.

Candy remembered exactly how to get there. How could she forget? They'd driven about an hour. She turned her headlights off and pulled behind the cinder block excuse for a store. She untied the van hatch and they pulled and pushed until the corpse smacked the gravel near the drainage pipe with a subdued thud.

"Get his wallet and his phone, Jo. I wiped down this wrench.

Here, hold it with this towel, hit him hard—the back of his head—and drop it. I'll turn the van around."

Jo knelt down and retrieved the wallet. The foul odor of bowel elimination by death was nauseating. She checked the other pockets and found his phone.

"OK, we can't stay here any longer. Keep his phone. Take any bills out and scatter them with the wallet, over there. Get his license, credit cards, anything with his name on it and give them to me. Smack him like I said."

"I can't hit him. I just can't, Candy. Why do we have to hit him?"

Candy got out of the van and took the wrench from her. Just go do the rest."

Jo tossed the wallet and a few dollar bills that were inside near the trail. As she got back in the van, it started raining hard and the wind picked up. She hadn't noticed the Club 654 paystub mixed in with the cash she'd thrown.

"What do we do now, Candy? How long before he's found you think? What if somebody saw us? Why did we put him there? Why did you hit him with that wrench?"

"Somebody else hit him with that wrench and killed him. Not me. Nobody saw us. And we want somebody to find him. I didn't wanna hit him either, Jo. I'm sorry you had to see it."

22

Hook, Line, And Sunk

Candy drove halfway home, then pulled over. "Jo, in the glove compartment, hand me the phone that's in there." Candy looked up "TL" in her phone contacts, then took the burner from Jo and placed the call.

"Hi, Tracy Lynne! It's Candy, hon. I'm feelin' better now. Let's hang out."

"Really, Candy? Yeah! Where you at? An' yeah, yeah, yeah, OK,OK,OK."

"I'm about an hour away and ready to hook up with you guys. Tell the guys to meet me behind the store in an hour. Tell 'em to wait for me there, OK? They got enough glass for me? I wanna try it, babe. Make sure they bring it."

"Want me to come, Candy?"

"No. You stay at the trailer. Get it all nice and ready for a party. You been up and down that path enough, right?"

"Yeah, great! I'm a clean it up. You'll see…yeah! Sam and Dave will meet you there." Tracy Lynne informed the brothers of their good fortune. Their prized piece wanted to hook up.

"Oh, yeah…Dave…we're gettin' some more of that girl! Remember…member?"

The brothers, Sam and Dave, had been awake for four days straight. The initial methamphetamine rush of thirty minutes they'd enjoyed four days ago was followed by the high, or shoulder as some referred to it, that lasted sixteen hours. They'd detail cleaned the wheels on the trailer and then disassembled two lawn tractors, a refrigerator, and a dishwasher on a dirt patch in front of their trailer. Somehow they had managed to finish the meth cook. The entire area surrounding the trailer held the toxic remains of their numerous one-pot meth production accomplishments. They'd argued for hours about how the finished stack of coloring book pages should be arranged and hung up inside on the trailer walls. Entering the end of their third day without sleeping or eating, they were desperate to find the euphoric initial rush, smoking bowl after bowl to no avail. The feelings of emptiness and the intense drug cravings increased with every passing hour. The meth was no longer working.

"When's she coming, Tracy Lynne, Tracy Lynne, Tracy Lynne?" they chanted. Tracy Lynne was still in the rush. She'd started smoking three days later than the brothers.

"About an hour or so. No hurry. Maybe it'll stop raining. You two gotta meet her up behind the store."

Candy was checking for a suitable location as she drove. She'd wiped off the blood spatter from her face with a Kleenex.

"I'm confused, Candy. You aren't really going to meet two guys back there. Are you? Are they the ones that attacked you? Who's Tracy Lynne? What should I do with all this?" Jo held up Erik's iPhone.

"No, of course not, Jo. I'm not meeting anyone. I'm counting on the 911 call. Tracy Lynne is who helped me escape from them. She was a sweet, decent person. Just fucked up on meth. I couldn't set her up to get arrested. She just needs help, maybe rehab, I don't know. Fuck those men. They deserve jail. They should pay for what they did to me. I'm sure they've done that to other women. Turn the phone off. We should've turned it off earlier. Take the sim card out. You know how? Then throw it out with his license. Got it?"

"Yeah, I know how. Got it."

23

Sleepover

"How about you stay with me tonight, Jo?" Candy parked in front of her house.

"Was hoping you'd ask. Not feelin' it… I mean, being alone… after all this. Thank you. Thank you for everything, Candy." Jo couldn't explain why she'd agreed to disposing of Erik's body so quickly. Maybe she didn't have enough time to react logically to Candy's swift action. Too late to worry about that now.

"Don't thank me, yet. Take the guest room, Jo." Candy limped off to her bedroom across the hall and threw herself onto her bed. Down pillows. Fleece blankets. Soft. Comfort. Sleep came swift and sure. For once the nightmares of her father's attacks behaved and missed their nightly appearance. While Candy slept, a text came in from Jim.

"Hey, hope you feel better. Text me or call when you get a chance."

24

The Mexico Room

"**H**ow you feeling, Scorp? We can stop and I'll give you a pill and take a look at your face and arms, if you want. Dressings should be changed."

"I could use a pill, Khloe. I'm hurtin' bad… my arms. There's a small town looks to be about three, four hours from my place. I spotted it on Google last night. Stick it in the Garmin. Let's stop and get a room there. Rest up." He looked over at her. Khloe seemed so relaxed. He'd never seen Candy that relaxed, he thought. Candy had an edge to her. He didn't think Khloe had a tough side to her personality like Candy. Maybe nursing had something to do with that? She was easy to be around. Her demeanor helped him relax. He wasn't feeling like he was in control. The searing pain and the uncertainty of the whole situation was getting the better of him. What would Candy do when she saw what he looked like? How would they open the vault now that the combination was lost? His payment for the stolen cars wouldn't come through from Dubai for weeks. How would he pay Abe and Jamey?

"OK, Scorp." Khloe was enjoying this last stretch of the trip. She'd never been to Tennessee. She loved what she'd seen so far. The fall weather was nice, helping improve her mood. She could hardly wait to see his house. Scorp hadn't described it and she didn't want to pry online. She thought it would be super nice. If he had enough money to pay her a fortune for a few days' work, it had to be magnificent. No comparison to her third-floor one-bedroom condo. At least she wouldn't have a mortgage soon. She was driving fast. The sun was streaming through the trees lining the highway that were first preventing, then allowing the rays to attack the windshield. They found a motel. The Brown's Motel sign read

Rooms of the World, Happy Birthday Moe, and *Low Monthly Rates.* Khloe registered and chose the "Mexico" room.

"I'm taking a quick soak, Scorp. You think you can clean up by yourself now? I could run the water for you when I'm finished." Khloe took her bag into the bathroom. She leaned out and smiled at him.

"Um…no, I can't move good enough. I could use your help. I'll be home soon an' my girl will take care of me, so this will be the last time you have to do it. I appreciate it, Khloe. You've been real nice to be around." Scorp hadn't been near a straight, citizen type woman, ever. He'd been abandoned as a child and grew up in foster homes. He dropped out of high school in the tenth grade. The girls he met in his teens didn't interest him. By the time he turned twenty-four he'd been recruited by Manic. The workload left no time for socializing and he wasn't much for that anyway. And then, he met Candy. And now Khloe. She had beautiful hazel eyes and silky blonde hair. A little tummy. She looked so healthy and happy. And she was sexy in a very natural way, he thought. Not flagrant. Subtle. Un-Candy-like. He was intrigued.

"Your turn, handsome. Get in here. Let's get those clothes off."

He was sound asleep. She sat on her bed and watched him sleep. He was beautiful, she thought. Taut stomach. Toned arms with just enough pop. Thick, long fingers with short, perfect nails. Her hands cupped her breasts. *Imagine.*

He'd been talking more. Explaining. Even asking her to be patient. The money was coming, he said. She'd see. A man of his word. *The money?* It wasn't as important to her now as it was at the start of the trip.as. Scorp, even damaged, was more *man* than any man she'd ever met.

She stood up and approached him. Close. So close she could hear the sheets rustle as his chest rose, then settled. Her hand reached up, inside her tee shirt, finding a swollen nipple. She looked up at the ceiling and exhaled. *When?*

25

Hitch A Ride

They had only driven a few hours when the call from Gina surprised them. After the call, Abe and Jamey returned to Annapolis in anticipation of meeting Gina the next day. They were hopeful she had additional information about Candise Doubleday. Anything at all that could help lead them to Scorp and their money.

At eleven, as planned, they met Gina at the restaurant. While ordering breakfast, Gina spoke. "I was hoping, maybe, me and Lily could, like, go with you two, to find Candy. I'll pay you three hundred dollars if we can go with you.

"Well, Gina, do you know exactly where Candis…Candy is?" Abe was scowling as he asked the question, his voice raised. He had no intention of traveling with a pregnant woman who looked like she was ready to pop and her brat, no matter how hot she was, if she couldn't tell him why they needed her. Jamey, however, was smiling, imagining how nice it would be having them along. A welcome distraction. He could only take so much of Abe and his sullen personality. Gina couldn't help but notice. Jamey had long sandy hair that was swept back and gathered into a short ponytail. His dark blue eyes crinkled when he smiled. He was smiling at her right now.

"Well, to be honest, I don't know exactly where she is. All I know is Tennessee. I do know if you need someone to introduce you to her, I'm that person. She is, like, well, not super friendly and can be very dangerous. And look, I know you two aren't insurance agents. Candy's never had anything worth insuring until now. Those suits and shoes you guys are wearing look ridiculous. And you need more makeup on your neck and hand tats. I can see spider webs." She reached over and helped Lily cut up her pancakes.

"So, like, I don't know what you want from her, but I can help you get whatever it is. And I get to see her."

26

Money For Nothing

Jim Griot, the owner of Essential Sales & Rental, was up early. He'd dreamed about the friendly young woman with the Jersey accent he'd met the night before at Club 654. At least they'd exchanged numbers.

He started his diesel Ford F-250 King Ranch pickup and drove to his eight o'clock appointment at Sunset Assisted Living. His parents were under the care of that facility. He parked, entered the glass walled lobby, and the odor of incontinence immediately filled his nostrils. He signed in and the receptionist directed him to the conference room.

"Good morning, Mr. Griot. Please, take a seat. We have a few incidentals regarding your account we need to resolve."

Jim sighed, put his coffee down, and sat down across from the beady eyed, white haired administrator. It wasn't the first time he'd sat opposite her. He hoped it would be the last.

"We must ask, Mr. Griot, that the total unpaid balance of your account be brought up to date immediately. As you can see, the outstanding balance due is $21,850. That covers two months in arrears and one month payable in advance. The entire amount is due now. As you'll recall, you signed a contract with Sunset Assisted Living that designates you as the responsible party." She pushed a copy of the contract and financial statement across the conference table.

"I'll see what I can do."

"Please don't delay, Mr. Griot. This needs to be taken care of immediately."

Jim left the building, sat in his truck, and watched a resident in a wheelchair feeding squirrels. He'd come back and visit his parents another day, soon. He'd get the money to pay the bill. He just needed business to pick up and then everything would be just fine. The monthly fees at Sunset Assisted Living were crazy high. And for the money, his parents got nothing. A cart in the hallway with their names stickered onto day-of-the-week pill organizers and one hot bath a week. The food was barely edible. He started the truck and drove to his next appointment. Maybe this meeting would be better.

Jim had agreed to meet auditors from Bank Two at Essential Sales & Rental. They were to verify heavy equipment inventory. On the way, he stopped at Double Donuts to pick up a box of coffee and a dozen donuts. He made his selections, paid, and stopped to pick up some extra napkins. He was juggling his purchases when his keys jangled as they landed on the tiled floor.

"Here, let me help you, Jim." It was Jo on the way in. She threw her scarf over her shoulder, crouched down, swooped up his keys, and handed them to him. "There you go. Let me get the door for you."

Jim had only seen Jo once, at Club 654 the other night, in months. They'd never talked about it; he suspected she had filed the formal EEOC complaint citing Essential Sales & Rental. He'd be meeting with his lawyer to discuss the complaint soon. Jo had resigned a week before Jim became aware of the formal letter outlining discriminatory practices and harassment filed with the Equal Employment Opportunity Commission.

"Thanks, Jo. Appreciate it." Jo held the door and walked over to Jim's truck, carrying the box of coffee he'd bought.

"No problem. How've you been, Jim?"

Jim sighed. "To be honest, I've been better. I sure miss you. You did a fantastic job with the inventory and payroll. Haven't found anyone to replace you. HR is working on it, but it's hard finding quality people like you, Jo. People who actually want to work, that is. How have you been? Have you found a job?" He suspected what had happened to cause Jo to file. He'd overheard some office gossip. He didn't know the details.

"Yeah, well, I got a job waitressing at the diner down on 43. It's not much, but the tips haven't been bad."

"That's good. Something will open up for you, you'll see."

"Thanks, Jim. You know, I enjoyed working with you, Jim. You always treated me with respect and kindness. I miss that. You're a good guy."

"Thanks, Jo. That means a lot. Hey, it was great getting to talk to you. You take care now."

"You too, Jim."

He was late for his second appointment. Jim roared out of the Double Donuts parking lot on his way to meet the auditors at his equipment yard. Luckily, he saw they hadn't arrived yet as he sped through the entrance gates. He hurried in and dropped off the donuts and coffee in the conference room, then went into his private office. Opening the top drawer of his desk, he retrieved his prescription and rattled out two Valium tablets and downed them with the last of his morning coffee.

"Good morning, Jim!" Laura, his office manager, was standing in the doorway. "I ran all the heavy equipment serial numbers you asked for. Here you go." She smiled and held the binder out. "If you need anything else, you know where to find me!"

Jim found Laura to be just a tad bit too perky for his liking. As if there were no problems that couldn't be solved with a smile. Her attitude annoyed him at times. This was one of those times. "Thanks, Laura. That's all I need right now." He grabbed a yellow highlighter and began studying the current inventory sheets.

His cell buzzed. It was the chief auditor. "Mr. Griot, this is Mr. Grim with Bank Two. I apologize. We are going to have to reschedule. Something's come up that requires our immediate attention. We'll touch base with you soon to set another date."

27

Welcome Aboard

"**We**'re going outside to talk about this, Gina. Come on, Jamey." The two bogus insurance agents left Gina and Lily, still eating breakfast and stood outside, under the Denny's sign.

"So, Abe, what do you think we should do? Should we take them with us to Nashville? I mean, I guess she could help us? Maybe negotiate? She knows them better than us. We don't know anything about Scorp's girlfriend."

Abe was pacing on the sidewalk. "Well, it can't hurt as long as we can control her. Not let her out of our sight, you know. Might be able to use them, one way or another."

"What do you mean by that, Abe? One way or another?"

"Let's just leave it at that, Jamey."

Abe opened the hatch on the Jaguar. Before they had left to look for Scorp, he'd loaded all the gear he might need should they find him. Sawed-off Browning shotguns, Tec 5000 sniper rifle, Glock 19 machine pistols, derringers, propane torch, duct tape, needle nose pliers, meat cleaver, razor blades, tweezers, baseball bat, sulfuric acid, and nylon rope. Abe rearranged the cargo. He covered everything with a blanket and put the rear seats up. While he was busy readying the SUV for their new passengers, Jamey made his way back to their table inside.

"OK, Gina, we are all in. You two are going with us."

Gina was glad it was Jamey, not Abe, who came back in. "Cool, but I've got a question. You aren't insurance agents and you aren't friends with Candy. So, why are you looking for her?"

"So we can find Scorp, Gina. He owes us money."

"Look, I know how Scorp makes his money, Jamey. So, you guys are, like, partners with him?"

"Yeah, you could say that."

"Oh, OK, I get it. He owe you a lot?"

Jamey looked over his shoulder to make sure Abe was still outside. "Over four hundred thousand, Gina. We acquired vehicles on his behalf and that's our share."

"I'm not good at math, Jamey, but Candy told me that Scorp only pays his crews two percent of the take. So it doesn't make sense that he hasn't paid up. It'd be like me stiffin' somebody a dollar." Jamey had never thought of it that way.

Gina reached in her coat pocket and pulled out a roll of bills. "Here, for takin' us."

Jamey held up his arms. "Don't need that. Put it away. You can get the check."

28

Ding Dong

Khloe woke up in the Mexico room of Brown's Motel and peeked out from under the covers. Scorp was sitting in the lone, stained plastic motel chair. He was partially dressed, sporting a sombrero decoration he'd snagged off their Mexico room wall.

"Very funny, amigo." Khloe was pleased he had a sense of humor. Pleased, and surprised at the same time. He'd been so serious the entire trip. For good reason, she thought, but still, it was good to see him lighten up.

"So it's time, Khloe. We'll be there today. You ready?"

"Sure, let's do it." Khloe wasn't sure she wanted the journey to end so soon. She would have a suitcase full of cash as her only company on the long ride home.

Scorp now remembered exactly what the house looked like. His memory of places and events prior to the accident was improving daily. "Set the cruise for seventy-five Khloe."

"OK, looks like it ain't that far till we get there."

They found the address with ease. Khloe pulled up next to the Miata that was parked near the front entrance. Scorp's house was no ordinary home, she thought. "Should I wait in the car?" Khloe's hands were clammy. Scorp's girlfriend was about to see her guy and it was going to be a shocker. And what would she do when she saw he was with another woman? How would Scorp explain that to Candy's satisfaction?

"I owe you. I couldn't have made it here without you." He reached over and touched her hand. "Don't worry about nothing, Khloe. It's all good. Get your bag. We'll stay here tonight." Scorp didn't know who owned the Miata, but he knew for sure Abe and Jamey wouldn't fit in it.

Scorp tried to open the front door. "At least she locked something." He didn't understand why Candy had left the entrance gates open. He tried the doorbell.

Candy jumped up out of bed. Jo was up now too and met her in the upper level hallway. They'd both been sleeping when the doorbell rang. "Come down with me, Jo. I have no idea who'd be coming here. Should have locked the gate last night. Forgot. She looked out the upstairs hall window. An old green Honda was parked out front.

"Don't you have a Ring, Candy?"

"Yeah, but it's still in the box." They rushed down the stairs and Candy looked through the peep hole. A man and a woman. She didn't recognize either of them. A pretty, young woman. One side of the man's face, ear and neck were covered with white gauze. "Jesus fucking Christ!" Candy stepped back from the door and guided Jo back and away.

"Open up Candy…it's me…Scorp." He stepped back and struggled to lift his arm up high so she could see the uncovered portion of the scorpions tattooed on his forearm. "See? It's me. I was in an accident and got burnt. This here's Khloe. She's a nurse. Helped me get home."

Candy looked through the peep hole again. She could see a portion of the tattoos. The rest of his arms were bandaged. And the voice? It was Scorp's gravely voice. It was him. She opened the door, stepped back, and they stepped in.

"What the fuck, Scorp. What happened to you? Candy moved closer and raised her arms. She wasn't sure he could be hugged in his condition. Scorp held his arms up slightly, and their hands met.

"I crashed. Suburban caught fire."

"Oh, God, that's awful. Lucky you weren't killed. Are you gonna be OK? I'm so sorry, Scorp."

"I think so, Candy. I'm getting better. It could have been worse. Lucky my eyes are OK. Couldn't remember much at first. I can get this fixed." He gestured to his face.

"You'll be OK, Scorp. I'm sure they can fix you up." Candy's initial shock subsided. She turned her attention to Scorp's new friend.

"And who's *this*?" Candy pointed forcefully at Khloe.

"Told you…Khloe. She's a travel nurse. Got me here. And who's *that*?" He pointed at Jo.

"This is Jo, Scorp. She's a new friend. She's been staying here to keep me company."

"Humph…."

Candy couldn't bring herself to hug him. She thought it would be painful for him. This wasn't the Scorp she knew. He looked sad and weak. He reached out slowly and touched her hand again. "I know I'm ugly now, Candy…an' I'm in a world of shit. Can we just sit down and talk this out? And what happened to you? You're all banged up too. What the hell?"

"I got caught up in something bad too, Scorp."

Khloe tried not to be obvious as she glanced at Candy and Jo. Candy was pretty, even with cuts and bruises. Jo was absolutely stunning. Khloe tried not to stare. Jo's makeup was perfect. Everything about her was perfect. Almost too perfect. There was something about her she couldn't put her finger on. Since they both had long robes on, Khloe couldn't judge their bodies well. She could see that Candy was petite and appeared to be built well. Jo was somewhat taller and her hair was longer.

Candy showed Khloe to the living room. "Take a seat. Me an' Scorp will be upstairs."

"I'm going up to your guest bedroom, Candy. I'll stay out of your way." Jo started up the stairs. She wasn't going to try to chat up Khloe, and she needed to get dressed. Candy didn't even look at her or acknowledge she'd said anything. Candy and Scorp took the elevator up to their bedroom. Candy sat on the love seat and Scorp settled on the edge of the bed.

"You first, Scorp. Tell me what happened."

"I was on my way to make a job payoff. Everything ran smooth. I just had to meet my crew and pay them. I don't remember what happened, but when I woke up I was in the hospital, all burnt up. They said I ran off the road and the Suburban caught fire. There was nothing left of it. Khloe was my nurse while I was in the hospital. I talked her into helping me get home. All my info was in my phone. It and the cash I had was burnt up, Candy. Abe and Jamey will be looking for me. I owe them some money." Scorp searched Candy's eyes. They were cold and calculating at times. This was one of those times. She crossed her legs carefully and pulled the robe close and tight.

"What happened to you, Candy?"

Candy stood up, turned around and hiked her robe up waist high. "I was just takin' a ride and stopped for some smokes. Next thing I knew I was captured by meth heads and they did this to me and a lot more. Managed to get away and back here." Scorp stared at the deep bruising around her panties. She had welts and deep scratches on her hips. Whoever did that to her was totally out of control, he thought.

"Jesus, Candy. I'll make them pay for touching you. Sons of bitches!"

"I already took care of that. So, how much you need to pay them off?" Candy dropped her robe down and turned back to face him, arms crossed. Anger was boiling inside. The accident wasn't Scorp's fault but it put everything they'd worked so hard for in jeopardy. If he had just stayed home with her none of this would've happened.

"Around nine hundred thousand." Scorp looked down. Candy knew. He always looked down when he was lying.

"Wow! So, you had all that on you?"

"Yeah, I did. So, Candy, how did you take care of *that*? The men that hurt you?" Scorp knew what she was capable of.

"Don't worry about that right now, OK? And nine hundred is a lot for one job. Why so much?"

"Well, umm……it was around four hundred seventy-five for the job, but I owe Khloe for helpin' me out, getting me home an' all."

"So, let me count…you owe her four hundred thousand for driving you home? What the fuck, Scorp? You mean to tell me you couldn't find someone to drive you here from wherever for less than that? That's crazy. How could you agree to do that?"

"Chrissakes, Candy, I lost everything. I didn't even have the house address. Had to research where we lived. Can't you see? She got me home and took care of me. She's been treating my burns. Making sure they're clean and covered up right. Givin' me…er…I didn't have anybody else…not even a phone, or your number. It's not a big deal. We got the money. What was I supposed to do? You tell me. I did what I had to do to get back home."

Candy wasn't going to mention that she tried to get into the vault while he was away. She'd sworn she'd never use the drugs stored inside. "All I got is the money in my backpack, so you'll need to open the vault." Candy looked away.

"I can't. The vault code was in my phone, Candy, and the phone melted along with my goddamn face." He didn't dare mention that he'd changed the combination before he left for the car theft job. Candy would be furious that he didn't trust her. And to change it once again the vault need to be opened first.

Candy knew he'd changed the combination. So he wasn't going to ask her to open the vault. Maybe she'd just let it play out. She changed the subject. "You're not staying here tonight with that bitch, though. Take her back to whatever motel you were staying in. We'll deal with this tomorrow. You can call the crew. Get it over with. Pay them and your new girlfriend and send her home. Guess you have their cell number, right?"

"Yeah, I have a thumb drive in the vault. It has their burner number on it. Look, she isn't a bitch, Candy. I wouldn't be here without her help. Leave her alone and she stays out of this."

"Whatever, Scorp. You sleep with *her* tonight." We open the vault tomorrow, then call your crew."

Scorp wasn't sure what he should do. The vault wasn't going to open. He'd have to tell the truth. He needed time to think.

"Whatever…yeah, whatever, Candy." He needed to spend some time with Khloe alone anyway. Explain the situation. Maybe he'd give Khloe what he could out of the backpack now and the rest later. He was sure Khloe would be patient. He was surprised he cared about what Khloe's reaction would be. She really didn't have a choice. Abe and Jamey? *That* was a problem. If he couldn't' come up with the cash, it would be war. His arsenal was in the vault.

Candy was so angry she couldn't think or see straight. Scorp changed the combination, messed up a job, and brought a woman home with him, agreeing to pay her a fortune, for nothing. And if they couldn't get the vault open, they'd all be in dead. Candy knew some members of the crews that Scorp used were cold blooded killers. She'd heard the stories. She shivered and directed Scorp to the bedroom door.

"Get out. Take her and go back to wherever you've been sleeping with her."

29

Messenger Girl

Jamey and Gina were trying to relax. Brown's Motel featured a tiny kiddie playground behind the office. They watched Lily trying out the sliding board and swing set.

"How are you feeling, Gina? That looks like it hurts." Jamey pointed.

Gina patted her stomach. "Nah, it's not that bad, really. The morning sickness I had, now that was bad. So, what are your plans, Jamey, once you get your money? Another car gig? Vacation?"

"I'd like to buy a house. I've never had one. I don't want to stay in this business. I have enough money. It's all invested. I don't need to do this type of work any longer. This was always gonna be my last job with Abe." Jamey realized he could go on for hours. Surely Gina would get bored, he thought.

"Sounds smart, Jamey. You like kids?"

"Love them. Thought you could tell." He looked over at the swing set. "I've got some nieces and nephews that I'm close with. Not the same as having your own."

"Yeah, suppose not. You know, you're a really nice guy, Jamey. A handsome man like you won't have any trouble finding a wife." Gina reached across the picnic table. Her hand rested on his.

While they were talking, Abe used the privacy he needed and transferred the cargo from the Jag to the Expedition. The tow truck would be arriving soon. He finished and texted Jamey.

"Playtime's over. Ge back here now."

"Oops, the recess bell has rung, Gina. Sister Mary Abe is calling me. Wants us back in class."

Abe tossed the fob to the Expedition to Gina." Go get the tank topped off. Take Lily with you and come right back."

"Yes sir, right away sir, anything else sir? Ding dongs or some fruit loops?" Abe's approach towards her was grating on her nerves. Hopefully this would be over soon.

"Humph…don't get smart with me. Just get going." Abe tilted his head toward the open motel room door. "Inside, Jamey. Here's the plan. We send Gina to Scorp's place. She knows them two. She can get in without a fight. Find out exactly what is going on. Come back and brief us."

"Isn't that dangerous, Abe? Will she be safe with them? Won't they get suspicious if she starts asking questions? I mean, we'll be lucky if they're still there. Don't want to scare them into running."

"Why wouldn't she be safe? They're her friends. The kid stays with us while she visits them two. And if they run, I'm gonna burn that house to the ground."

Gina was navigating the Quick Mart lot to secure a spot to fill up when an old man backed out of a parking space right in front of her. She slammed on the brakes and avoided a collision. Her panic stop caused Abe's cache of deadly force to slide around, clinking and clanking loudly. While she was gassing up, she opened the hatch to see what had caused all the commotion behind her. She pulled a blanket aside. Abe was prepared, she thought. He'd better be.

30

Healin' Feelin'

"Do you know any clinics around here, Jo?" She hadn't forgotten what Tracy Lynne said about the meth heads. She needed to be checked for disease. All those years with men and she'd never even got crabs, she thought. And now she could be infected. "And I got a loose tooth too. I need a dentist."

"I have a doctor I go to, Candy. Real smart and nice. She's accepting patients. I'll call her office and get you an appointment. OK? I don't know a good dentist around here. We could use one."

"I guess your doctor is cool. I've never been to a doctor, Jo. I don't have insurance. Can I just pay cash?"

"Yeah I'm sure you can. I'll call her now." Jo got Candy an appointment for the following morning. Jo was astonished. Candy'd never been to a doctor.

Candy filled out the forms as best she could while Jo sat with her in the waiting room.

"You feeling better, Candy? You're walking better. Still sore?"

"Little sore, but, yeah, I'm a lot better. I really appreciate you getting me in here, Jo. I'm a little scared. Can you go in with me?"

"They wouldn't let me do that, Candy. You'll be fine. She couldn't be nicer, you'll see."

"Hi, Miss Doubleday? I'm Dr. Mondousha." She reached out and shook hands with Candy.

"So, how did it go, Candy?" Jo looked over at Candy as they drove back.

"Good, I guess. She had a lotta' questions. Put my answers in her laptop. Then she sent me down the hall and somebody took blood. Said she wants me to see a gynecologist."

"She say why?"

"Cause I've never been to one."

Jo didn't know how, or if she could respond to that.

"The doctor looked me over and frowned a lot. Asked me if I'd been in a fight. I told her no. Didn't think she needed to know that."

"Yeah, doctors have to report assaults if they suspect. But your bruises and cuts are way better…right?"

"Yeah, they've faded but I'm sure she saw some of them. My boobs are still that orange color bruises get, you know, like after the black and blue goes away."

They got back to Candy's house and Jo parked the Miata in the garage. Candy made sure the entrance gates were closed and locked. Scorpio and his new "girlfriend" couldn't just drive up the next time they decided to visit. They'd have to use the call box on the entrance gates. Candy was curious. Was he sleeping with her? She was pretty, but not built that well. Looked like a good girl. Good girls weren't Scorp's type. At least the Scorp she used to know wasn't attracted to the girl next door. If any girl would be Scorp's good girl, it was going to be her, not Khloe. She'd always trusted Scorp. They'd been apart…yet faithful, for years. The sex they both had with Gina and the clients she'd serviced for cash didn't register as unfaithful. Maybe she was jealous of Khloe? Was her new life being threatened?

"Look at the sky! Awesome isn't it, Candy?" The late fall sky was purple, white, and orange. Stratified, repeating color wisps. "I just love being here. Everything about this house is just perfect. Is this really Scorp's house? Just doesn't fit him, you know? How long are you staying here?"

Candy opened the door and turned to Jo. "It's cold, Jo. Let's get in and we can talk later."

Candy was feeling better. She needed to freshen. She turned the huge waterfall on. Bodywash. Everywhere. Her hands glided down, up, lifting, flicking. Front. Back. She double soaped and slid two fingers in, slightly. Out, in, slide, press. Jo's emerald green eyes, full lips and blonde locks mesmerizing her mind. Yes, she was feeling much better. *When?*

"Hello?" It was Scorp on Khloe's phone. Candy was drying off.

"I spotted them where we're staying, Candy. Abe and Jamey. The dudes I owe. They have Gina and Lily with them. And Gina is pregnant. I can't believe it. They're staying here at the Brown's Motel. I saw them go into the motel office. No way they followed us here. They must not know we have a room here too. Sure you won't let us stay at the house? Candy? Candy? You there?…Candy?"

"Here's one, Scorp. It's closer to your house." Khloe showed him the ad on her laptop for the Streamside Inn.

31

Open Sesame No

"**O**pen up, Candy." Scorp and Khloe were at the front door. They'd parked outside the gates and climbed the side fence. Candy wasn't answering his phone calls and the call box on the gate was turned off. They'd packed up and left, skipping the check-out process. Scorp wasn't giving up. He had to somehow get the vault open. Their lives depended on it.

Candy and Jo had heard a car approaching and flipped on the perimeter security cameras. Jo had spent the night. They saw the old green Honda park and watched as Scorp struggled to make it over the six-foot fence. He fell off and landed in the tall grass inside the fence and lay still with Khloe hovering over him for what seemed like an hour until he finally got to his feet.

Candy opened the door. "Family room, Scorp". Candy was livid. He'd ruined everything. And why? Because he hadn't trusted her.

"What about her?" Scorp half pointed to Jo.

"What about *her*?" Candy pointed to Khloe.

"Jo, could you grab us some coffee? You know what, Scorp? They both stay and hear this. We're all in the same shit storm right now, so no secrets."

Khloe had expressed her fear of Candy. Scorp told her not to worry. He would handle her. Just be quiet. Khloe didn't think Scorp could handle anyone just yet. He could barely tie his shoes. And despite her looks and stature, there was an aura surrounding Candy. Khloe recognized trouble when she saw it. And Candy was trouble. Scorp was so appreciative of anything Khloe did for him. Like no other patient she'd ever nursed. Khloe thought it might be because no one had ever treated him well. She was hoping he was attracted and liked her. She wanted to know everything about him but didn't want to push too hard. He was talking to her and sharing a little. His eyes told her he was grateful. They'd become somewhat intimate mentally, she thought. He couldn't smile but his eyes communicated. He'd been so lucky the fire hadn't destroyed his vision. They had the same goal. Get him back into shape. She'd talk to him about skin grafts and plastic surgery once things settled. He needed to know there was no reason he couldn't look better. He had the money it would take. She'd seen what those doctors could do. Scorp would be just fine.

"So, Scorp, let's go down and get the vault open."

Scorp fidgeted. He gulped. "I changed the combination before I left, Candy. It was the new combination that was in my phone. Thought you might use while I was gone. I know I shouldn't have done that." Scorp had decided he may as well just tell her. Waiting wouldn't make the situation better.

Candy paced. She lit a Newport. "You changed the vault numbers before you left? Didn't trust me? How can you *not* trust me. After all we've been through? I'm the only person you should trust, Scorp. So we're fucked. And you got some kinda shit going on in your 'tool room' I wanna know about. Don't trust me about that too?"

Khloe watched and listened. It was clear that Scorp and Candy cared for each other. It was also obvious that they were experiencing a crisis so serious their relationship might not survive it.

"Yeah, I changed it. I was worried you'd start using. I didn't want to see that happen, Candy. That's why. You've been clean. I was gonna change it back as soon as I got home, but it has to be open to make the change. The tool room is a bitcoin operation I had set up. It could be a money maker. I paid a guy to install it. I don't know all how it works. I need to contact him and see where we're at with it. I don't have his number either. And I was gonna tell you about it once I made some money off it."

"Jesus Christ, Scorp! We have all the money we need. And no

way to get to it. Killers looking for us. No weapons. No backup. Nothing. We're all gonna die because a you. And they got Gina and Lily. How the fuck did that happen? You tell them where she was? How else would they have found her?"

"I don't know how they found her. And I don't know why they have her and the kid. Doesn't make sense. Unless…."

"Unless *what*? I won't let anything happen to her, Scorp. We go back too far. Can't happen. We have to get her away from those bastards."

"I'm not ready for a battle with them two, Candy."

"Me neither, Scorp. We might not be able to avoid it. And I got more questions about your tool room. What is bitcoin? How is that helping us? Why did you hide it from me? Thought I was too stupid to understand it?"

"Like I said, I don't understand the whole thing, but it's some kind of math thing you get points or cash for… I don't know. It sounded real good when he explained it all to me. I'll find my guy if I can and see what's goin' on with it."

"Alright. I'll let it go. For now. I don't see why you all of a sudden hide stuff from me. I guess the bitcoin isn't important right now. Can you call the guys that put the vault in for help getting it open?"

"It's not that easy, Candy. It was bought through three shell companies. Installers can't help. Don't know who could except the factory. Not sure how long it would take. I'd have to go through the shells."

"You finished the car job, right? How much did you make on the job, Scorp? Just use that to pay everybody."

"Near thirty million. I won't see that until delivery is done. It'll take weeks to get paid. It's always like that, Candy. You know all my business is export."

Jo and Khloe looked at each other, then looked away. The conversation Candy and Scorp were having was beyond confusing. They had so many questions that couldn't be asked. At least couldn't be asked now. They could feel and see the tension. Jo was seeing more of Candy in control. It was exciting. Candy had told her it was a "friend's" house. She'd ask about that when the time was right. It had to be Candy's house as well as Scorp's.

Khloe felt sorry for Scorp. Candy was being super harsh. She wanted to help. But how? The situation was complicated and her field of study hadn't covered anything close to this. She knew one thing. The last week or so was far more stimulating than working the graveyard shift at Holy Savior. She felt *alive*. Even with Candy talking about vaults, bad guys, and bitcoin. And thirty million dollars? What was Scorp exporting?

"What about a burner bar, Scorp ? You told me it'd get the vault open. Can't we do that? We gotta do something. We can't just sit here waiting for them to find us." Candy was pacing.

"I know…I know. We'd have to find a burner bar and someone who knew how to use it. And I don't know how much time we have. Abe and Jamey aren't that far away. If they know where we live, they could be here today. Don't know. We need to get outta here and hide somewhere if we don't get it open soon, Candy."

"Great. Fuckin' great, Scorp." Candy motioned for Jo to follow her upstairs. "I'll work on finding a burner bar. You take your girlfriend and get the fuck out. Find yourselves another one-star and stay there." As much as she loved Scorp, he'd pushed her to her limit.

"OK, we'll be at the Streamside Inn."

Candy took Jo by the hand and led her into her bedroom, then locked the door. Jo was so curious. She couldn't help herself. She had to know.

"I am just so upset, Jo. I wanted to hug him so bad when I first saw him, but I'm so sore and he is so burnt up. I don't know how to fix this."

"Who's Gina and Lily, Candy? And is this your house, or his? And what's that about 'using'? Hope you don't think I'm being nosy. Well, I guess I am. I'm just concerned. For you. For us."

Candy wanted to tell Jo everything. Her new carefully planned life shredded. Blown up. And Gina, so near and in trouble. After the Erik disaster, she knew Jo could be trusted. Their lives bound together by his death.

"Gina's my best friend. To be honest, we were lovers. She's a single mom and Lily's her daughter. She's around three years old, I guess. We lived together for a few years, near Annapolis. Things were great between us until she had a baby. Things were still good with us after that, just different. I can't believe she's near here. I never thought I'd see her again. I think about her every single day. An' yeah, this house is mine and Scorp's. I wasn't in a good place back then, Jo. My life, I mean. Scorp 'n me worked together to get away from all the problems we had. Most caused by my father. He's dead now. We moved here thinkin' we could start out fresh, together. Scorp was talkin' about drugs when he said that about me using. I got a past with drugs, Jo. I wasn't hooked on heroin or nothin' like that. I'm off the shit now."

Jo patted the bed and Candy sat next to her. "My God, Candy. I'm so, so sorry. I feel partly responsible for messing up your plans. You know, with Erik and all. How can I help?"

"I don't know, Jo. That fuckin' vault is the problem. You have any idea where we can find special tools? That might help us. We need a burner bar setup and somebody who knows how to use it. The vault has millions inside. All Scorp's weapons. An' a shit load of drugs. Not for me. I'm selling them."

"Who are the people looking for Scorp?" Jo wanted to ask *where* all the money and drugs came from. Not the time to ask. "And what is a burner bar?"

"It's guys Scorp owes money to lookin' for him. He missed a payoff when he had the accident. A burner bar is a super torch that'll cut through anything. I've never seen one or know how it works. Jo, I'm sorry you're mixed up in this. You're stuck with us until...."

"Until what?"

"Until we kill the creeps coming for Scorp, or they kill us. Our only way out is inside the vault."

"I might know someone who could help us, Candy."

32

Ta Ta Troubles

The drive from Annapolis to the outskirts of Nashville took much longer than expected. Abe was not happy with the number of stops they'd made along the way. The women aboard were slowing them down considerably. Gina kept Lily occupied with an old V-Smile game that Audrey had given her. Abe had announced they would get a motel outside of Nashville. He was incensed that what should have taken a day had taken three. They needed a break and time to pinpoint Scorp's location. He checked them into Brown's Motel—*Rooms of the World*. The sign read *Under New Management, Pick your Country* and *Free Wi-Fi*. Abe picked the Egypt room and the Australian room. They'd all gone into the motel office. Lily couldn't wait until they got their rooms. She'd had to go potty for an hour, so she used the lobby bathroom. When they walked out, Abe noticed a couple across the motor court packing up an old green Honda. One side of the man's face, neck, and upper arms were bandaged. The woman with him was doing all the work. After loading the trunk, she got in the driver's side. Odd couple, he thought.

The foursome carried their bags into their respective rooms and met at the truck as planned. They needed to find some food. Jamey hit the start button. The Jag rumbled to life and stalled. The Incontrol display screen was blank. Dead. Jamey looked at Abe. He hit the start button again, hoping for a reboot. That had worked one time a month ago. The Jaguar wasn't cooperating.

"One moment, ladies. Let me have a word with my partner." Abe and Jamey got out and walked across the parking lot.

"What the fuck, Abe? Why did you buy this lemon? It looks good an' all, but we need something reliable. And this ain't the first time. They can't fix it! Incontrol? Them engineers at Ta Ta should've named it Nocontrol. The first time this happened they had to give you a whole new ride. Jesus, what a piece of shit. What do we do now?"

"Yeah, I know. Should of bought a Honda. Or a Toyota. Must still be makin' the control panels in England. People with bad teeth and shaky fingers tryin' to be techies."

"So, what should we do, Abe? Bet the closest dealer is in Nashville. And we got all the weapons an' shit in the back."

"Yeah, I know. My bad. Just liked the looks of it. I'll trade it once we get through this. We can Uber to a rental car place, get an SUV and have the Jag towed."

"That ain't good. I mean, the rental. In our name? Not cool, Abe."

"Use your alter ego, Jamey. Use your head."

Abe tried to explain the problem to Gina in simple layman's terms. "Truck is broken down, Gina. We're going to need to have it towed and get a rental."

"Is it the Incontrol, Jamey? I saw the black screen. I've heard about that problem Jags have. Me and Candy had a Jag once. Nothing but repair bills. Give you a plastic Jag pen when you pay. Couldn't get Triple A to tow us after awhile. They cut us off. Too many tow jobs."

"Yep, that's the problem. We'll get a rental. It's going to be Uber Eats tonight. Not sure how all this is going to set us back timewise." Jamey was thrilled. Gina knew about cars!

"I've waited so long to see Candy, Jamey. A while longer won't hurt."

Abe and Jamey Ubered to the only car rental agency they could find. Jaguar of Nashville would be sending a rollback for the SUV but couldn't bring them a loaner or any information on a fix and return date.

"We'll take anything but a Jaguar." The fat man behind the counter looked up and over his thick, dirty glasses. "Ain't gotta worry about that, son. Ain't a Jaguar SUV within a hundred mile a here. I got a Ford Expedition, four wheel drive. It will haul, tow and go anywheres. Great for hunting. Gas hog though. Three ninety-five a week. Return it with a full tank. You want it?"

"Perfect. We're gonna be doing some hunting." Jamey offered a stolen credit card, fake Florida license and filled out the papers. They did the walk around and confirmed it would work.

Abe drove. Jamey stared out the window. It felt like time had stopped. He was thinking about Gina. Her swollen stomach. Breasts. Lips. He'd talked to her before they left to get the rental. Sparkling eyes. Porcelain complexion with a rose tint. Thick blonde hair. She was stroking her baby belly as they chatted. Jamey sensed she had secrets. Hidden down deep. There was a sadness about her. When she talked to him her eyes never left his. She would sway side to side, rubbing her stomach. Her other arm herding Lily, who was scrambling to get free. Gina had a slow, yet un-Southern cadence when she talked. As if she was measuring each syllable before it escaped. He wanted more than talk. *When?*

33

Love Hurts

Candy was on her side, naked and covered by silk sheets from the waist down. The early morning sky was producing an eerie other-world haze that snuck through her bedroom blinds and bathed the room softly. She'd gone to bed early. Thought-exhausted. The only thing that had felt good the past few days was throwing Scorp and Khloe out. That and having Jo stay over.

Jo crept across the hallway, turned the lever slowly and cracked Candy's bedroom door. She could see Candy's breasts. Compressed. Spilling out under arm. Her slow, steady breaths expanding her ribbed back, causing her exposed nipple to glide on silk. Bright pink on black. Jo tiptoed in. Sliding up close, she spooned. Touching Candy's arm softly .Candy's hair stood on edge. Reflex. Jo reached around and placed her hand. Palm to flat midsection rising and falling rhythmically. Candy's skin twitched horse-like to repel the intrusion. Unconscious reaction. Jo leaned closer. Candy's scent enveloping her. She slink-slid back. Off. Out. Silently. Door closed. Looking up, she exhaled. *When?*

34

Sleepin' And Dreamin'

Scorp and Khloe found a motel minutes from his house, nestled in a valley with a small stream running alongside. The Streamside Inn would be their home tonight.

Scorp was sleeping. Dreaming. The vault was open and Candy and he were tossing fistfuls of thousand-dollar bills over their heads, laughing. Khloe was naked, skipping wildly and catching the bills as they floated in air.

Khloe dried off. Body spray. Purple thong. XL tee shirt…hanging…just below. She giggled quietly. A "turtle shirt," as her girlfriend at work called it. Two inches below the snapper. She looked out and saw that Scorp was asleep, on his good side. She sat on the bed and watched him. His arms. Just the right amount of pop. Thick, long fingers with short, perfect nails. Her hand cupped her breast. *Imagine.* He'd been talking more. Explaining. Even asking for her to be patient. The money was coming, he said. She'd see. A man of his word.

He and Candy were bickering. Maybe they always argued? Or was it the situation? That would cause any couple to fight, she thought. She could hear him breathing. The rise and fall of his chest rustling the sheets. She slid her hand up inside her tee shirt, finding a swollen nipple. She looked up, then exhaled. *When?*

35

Body Of Evidence

Bob and Bobby took the call. They were twenty minutes out. Both were veterans with the Tennessee State Police. Actually Bob and Bob. Too confusing, so one gave in and was known as Bobby. Not tremendously less confusing. They even looked alike. Portly, short, and broad shouldered. The 911 call said there was a body. Behind the store. *That* store. The store they'd visited more than a few times. The woman who owned it called 911 now and then when her sons got out of line and stole candy, cigarettes, or sodas. Sometimes a neighborhood alcoholic peeing or pooping in public. A cat up in a nearby tree. But a dead body? Never.

They drove around to the back of the crumbling convenience store carefully, avoiding giant rain filled holes as best they could. "What we got here, Bobby? This is as dead as they get. Look at that arm stickin' out. Looks like he's hitchhiking." Fighting relentless rain, the two State Troopers put their patrol car's high beams on, then slopped through the mud gravel mix to get a closer look at the body. Short black hair. About five foot nine. Medium build. Khakis. Long sleeve button down shirt. No jacket. Timberland boots. The young man face down in the mud appeared to be too clean cut to have lived anywhere nearby.

"Check his pockets, Bob. See that big wrench? Leave it. Let's walk around. See if we spot anything else."

"Looks like a bunch a tracks, Bobby. Tire tracks, shoe tracks. Even with all the rain I can see them. Them boys got a trailer down that trail, remember?" Bob pointed to the ragged path.

"Yeah, I remember, Bob. Real nice place they got down there. That's the second one they've had. First trailer blew up during a meth cook about five, six years ago. Too bad it didn't blow them up with it. They'd been better off. I could never figure how they got them trailers way back in them woods, Bobby. Looks like you'd need a copter to place them down there." He exhaled and the smoke from his cigar quickly dispersed as it mixed with wind and rain.

"Looky here, Bobby." Bob bent over with a loud grunt and picked up a wallet, a few one dollar bills, and a paystub. The bushes nearby had preserved them from the rain. They backtracked under the wide eaves of the store, trying to stay dry. "I'll bag these before they float away."

Bob lit a new cigar. "Damn, no license in his wallet. Always makes everything harder. Wait, this paystub says Club 654, Bobby. Erik Stryker, employee number thirteen. Not much cash. No credit cards. Maybe a robbery."

"No car here, Bob. Maybe a carjacking? You think them trailer boys had anything to do with this?"

"I don't know, Bobby. Guess we might end up talking to them."

"Got any crime tape, Bob?"

"Nope."

They retreated to their respective cars. Bob called dispatch and reported in, then hurried over to Bobby's car. "OK, Bobby. We got at least an hour or two. Let's Fortnite." They had pulled their cruisers to the far side of the lot behind the store and turned their headlights off. An eerie glow from two phones pierced the tinted patrol car windows.

36

Fight Or Flight

"**W**here could they be, Syd? I mean, I thought they might have gone for a walk but it's been hours. I'm worried. I'm checking Gina's room."

Audrey went in. "Syd, Come here! She's gone. Look, see, Lily's favorite stuffed animal is missing and her backpack isn't here."

"OK, *OK*, Audrey. Calm down, calm down. Let's sit down and think about this. She may have taken Lily to a playdate or sleepover and forgot to tell us, or we forgot."

"I didn't forget a playdate or a sleepover, Syd." Then she saw it. A note on Gina's bed.

"Look, Syd." She picked up the note.

"Thanks for letting us stay with you. I have decided to be on my own. Lily and I and the baby will be good. I am sorry if this is a shock. It shouldn't be. Gina."

Syd put his hand on her shoulder. "Let's give it until tomorrow. She might change her mind and come home. If she doesn't, we can make some calls. My bet is she's going to try to hook up with her friends in Tennessee."

"She won't get away with this, Syd. She's carrying your…our baby."

Audrey sobbed over her bagels with cream cheese in the morning. "Maybe we should have treated her better, Syd. You know, I mean, bought her a car or started a college fund for the girls?"

"Yeah, maybe so, maybe so. Too late now. Appears they won't be coming home. I'm not sure what we can do. We don't have any legal rights. We don't even know her last name. I know it can't be what she told us…Smith."

Audrey composed herself. "Let me make some calls, Syd. I have a few ideas. She is *not* getting away with this."

Audrey Googled "private investigators near me." She found a local woman who advertised that she had extensive missing person experience. She made the call and set up an appointment.

"Hello, Kate Finder? My name is Audrey Abrams. This is my husband Syd." The private investigator agreed to see them immediately. "We are trying to find a woman and her three-year-old who were living with us for the past year. She left two days ago. She told us her last name was Smith but we are sure that was a lie. It wasn't important to us until now. She's eight months pregnant, maybe a few weeks more. We didn't have any idea she was unhappy living with us."

"OK, could you please fill out this questionnaire, Mrs. Abrams. That will give me some facts that may help me locate her."

Audrey looked at the questions. "I don't have answers to any of these questions. Gina didn't have a driver's license or bank accounts, friends, family…nothing. Well, there is one friend. Syd thinks she left to hook up with her, in Tennessee. We know her first name is Candy, or Candise. Lived with Gina across the street from us before she moved in with us. We don't know her last name either. Candise had a boyfriend? I guess he was a boyfriend. His name is Dr. David Haspert. He is a local cosmetic dentist. He might know something?"

"Great. That will help. I've seen Dr. Haspert's commercials. He has a new procedure he's promoting. I will approach him and see if he can provide some information on Gina. Do you have a picture of Gina and her daughter?"

"Sure. I'll text you some pics."

"I can start on this tomorrow. I need to request a five hundred dollar retainer."

37

Chickens And Spiders

The brothers plodded up the rocky, muddy path. Tracy Lynne was thrilled. Super focused on her objective—hook up with Candy. She'd been captivated, enchanted by petite blonde women since she was in elementary school. She wanted Candy to herself. Her inability to control her impulses had prevented her from concealing Candy's phone call a little longer from Sam and Dave. She'd divulged it before thinking, and now she had to hurry and clean up the trailer to prepare for Candy's visit. The chemicals causing massive dopamine release in her brain were also clouding her judgment. She'd stayed at the trailer as Candy had asked. She was scrubbing everything in sight. She covered the engine parts on the kitchen table with clean sheets. She threw a comforter over the bloody mattress. The trailer had to be perfectly clean when Candy got there.

Dave, the younger brother, was struggling. Sam and Dave were nearing their fifth sleepless day. At the trailer a short while ago, they were both seeing the shadow people. The "people" who frequently haunted meth addicts. They had scurried around the trailer covering up all of the windows in the trailer, hoping to eliminate the hallucinations.

On the path, their delusions worsened. Sam was convinced huge orange chickens were following him. They would draw near, pecking at his heels. He tried to stop them, kicking crazily and kept falling down. Dave helped him up a dozen times or more. Sam was trying to verbalize what was happening. It wasn't working. Dave had his own problems. Furry black widow spiders lined the path. Their eyes were glowing red. The spiders were fast, scrambling everywhere. Some crawled up and inside his jeans. He smacked and

119

killed them before they could bite him. Sam could hear loud slaps on wet jeans behind him. With their personal battles hindering progress, it took an hour for the duo to reach their objective.

38

Wait ... What?

"**W**ait…What? Bobby, you see that?"

"Yeah." Bob turned on the high beams, chirped the siren, and they idled across the parking lot. "What the heck. It's those trailer freaks. They're messing with our victim!"

The tweakers, Sam and Dave, tumbled out of the woods and were staggering around aimlessly. Sam and Dave danced around the corpse, arms outstretched, flailing away, wailing in some unearthly tone. Dave picked up the large open end wrench he'd seen poking out of a puddle. Somewhere in his head he thought they might be able to use it disassembling equipment. They collided with each other, fell down, and landed in a heap near the bathroom door at the rear of the store.

Bob and Bobby vaulted out of the cruiser. They cuffed the brothers quickly and helped them move over against the wall of the store, out of the rain. They guided them to seated positions and zip tied their ankles. Bob searched their pockets, finding clumps of crystal meth and two glass pipes. They shook off some of the rain and jumped back into the patrol car.

"Those two men are fading out, Bob. Bet they haven't eaten or slept for days. I've seen that vacant look before. Their binge is done. Not worth talking to them until they recover, if they recover. Fair amount of them don't get better once they go that far. End up crazy until they die."

"Time to check in with Mr. Gold Buckle, Bobby." That was Bob's nickname for their boss, Corporal Creed, who was notorious for wearing his special gold belt buckle that signified his rank, showing the world just how important he was.

Bob, you know, it's really a shame. He pointed to the hapless pile leaning against the store. My wife works at Community House, you know, the rehab center. Just a part time receptionist there. She comes home with stories. You'd think opioids would be the big problem. Opioids are big, but crystal meth is worse. She says over half of the tweakers relapse. I blame the system, Bob. We can't get ahead of this the way we go about it. I mean, look at them two. They need help, not jail. Might be good people inside those fucked up bodies.

"Geez, Bobby, going soft on me?"

"Not soft. Smart. We can knock out the labs. Tennessee has done a great job with the meth labs here. Ain't near as many as a few years ago. That's great but now the Mexican cartels are dumping tons of the shit here, and everywhere else. Stuff is cheaper and higher quality than homegrown. Don't know how we can stop it. We seize a truckload and there's another one right behind it. God Damn shame is what it is. Then we lock up the heads. Yeah, we have to if they get violent, break the law. I get that. I'm a cop. It just doesn't help them. The drug is just too fucking addictive. They can't stop. It's worse than heroin. I mean, look over there at them two. Their faces, teeth, and bodies. Chemicals oozing out of 'em."

"OK, OK, Bobby, you done with your soapbox speech? We all got problems."

Bob called dispatch and requested transport for two meth overdoses. Homicide would make the decision about charging them with murder once, or if, the two men survived and were coherent. They'd be held on possession for now. Bob then summoned a coroner and asked to speak to Corporal Creed.

39

Counting CATS

"**M**r. Griot? Paul Grim with Bank Two here. I'd like to schedule our postponed inventory audit for tomorrow at 8 a.m."

"Yes sir, Mr. Grim. Not a problem. I'll see you then."

The next day, Jim made his habitual daily stop at Double Donuts on his way to meet the bank auditors. The young man who took his order was unusually chatty. Jim had ordered through him several times in the past two weeks and he'd never uttered a word except "my pleasure" when Jim thanked him. He was a new employee.

"Hey mister, wasn't it you who dropped your keys, what, last week, trying to juggle a big order? That girl that helped you. She your girlfriend?"

"Ha, no, no, she used to work for me, that's all. She caught your eye, huh?"

The cashier feigned embarrassment. "Guess so. She was real pretty." He'd waited on the attractive blonde with the red scarf several times. He thought she was the perfect woman. The right look, height, and weight. She'd never, ever looked at him when she ordered and paid. Always parked right at the front door, he'd watched her get in her sports car and check her makeup in the rear view mirror.

"She's real smart too. Need to borrow your restroom, what's it, Quinn?" Jim read his name tag. He'd never paid any attention to him. Always just ordered and paid.

"Yeah, it's Quinn. Sure, key is back there, hanging up. Just be sure to put it back. I'm on break." Quinn took his apron off, rounded the sales counter, and pushed the glass doors to the shop open. He'd seen Jim's pickup before but had never needed to get a close look. Finding Jim's F-250 five rows over, he used his phone and took pictures, capturing *Essential Sales & Rental*, the address, phone number and website.

Double Donuts was the tenth job Quinn had since dropping out of high school in his senior year. His grades had been deplorable. Quinn was a loner. No friends in school. He'd been suspended for breaking into lockers twice. He lied about his home life to counselors. When his lies caused problems for others, he blamed them for being stupid and believing him. He was twenty-six now. All of his classmates had gone to college, joined the military, or had real jobs. He felt humiliated when he recognized guys he had known in high school waltzing into Double Donuts with hot girls, buying lattes with platinum American Express cards.

His identical twin brother, Erik, had similar difficulties. His grades in school were poor. He'd been caught stealing money and credit cards from fellow students. After barely graduating he couldn't hold a job. He tried working for Lyft. It lasted two weeks. He wasn't cut out for such close interaction with the public. When the job at Club 654 appeared on Craigslist, he applied. No background or drug testing. Just show up and look at driver's licenses. It helped pay the bills.

Mr. Grim and two junior auditors met Jim in his office. Jim got there half an hour early and downed two Valiums with his morning coffee. The heavy equipment inventory binder that Laura, his office manager compiled for him was on his desk. It wasn't well done. He sighed as he remembered how well Jo managed to handle jobs like this. It contained serial numbers for every piece of equipment in the yard, as well as model numbers, brief descriptions, arrival date, and sale/lease dates where applicable. "Would this help you, Mr. Grim?" Jim offered up the binder.

"No thanks. We have our own paperwork we have to match and fill out. This is going to take quite some time. Possibly a week. You have over four hundred items financed with us, correct?"

"Sounds right, I guess. I concentrate on moving it, not counting it."

"Well, we'd better get started. We'll be back every day until we're finished."

Essential Sales & Rental was the largest distributor of CAT brand diesel equipment in Tennessee. They sold, rented, and serviced CAT and various other lines. Jim had ordered forty midsize CAT front end loaders. They were shown correctly on the books as bank owned inventory subject to audit. The average cost for one was three hundred thousand dollars. Twelve million dollars inventory value in that one line item alone. He'd sold one without removing it from the ledger. Made a cash deal with a wealthy contractor north of Nashville. Sold it for one third of its value. That CAT loader was then shown as a rental on the inventory spreadsheet. The infusion of cash from the sale floated his business for another month. The money from the sale was used to pay back taxes, building lease payments, and payroll. He wanted to make sure his loyal employees continued to be paid. They had all helped him build the business. He wasn't going to let them down.

"OK, then. Suppose you know what's what out there?"

"Sure do. We'll be sending you a report of our findings when we are finished. We're backed up right now, so it may be a while before you see it in your inbox."

Jim was relieved to hear the auditor's report would be slow in coming. He grabbed his coat. "I have another appointment, gentlemen. Coffee and donuts are in the conference room. If you need anything, my office manager, Laura, will be happy to help you. She's right down the hall." Jim rushed out to his truck. His appointment with his lawyer was in forty minutes.

"Did I hear my name?" Laura swooped into Jim's office.

"Oh, hi Laura. This is Mr. Grim. He's with the bank. I was just telling him you would be available today if he had any inventory questions." Laura was nice looking, Jim thought, but what a pain in the ass.

"Why, of course! Whatever you need, Mr. Grim. Happy to

help!"

Paul Grim was thirty-nine. He had married his high school sweetheart and they had four children and one on the way. Laura had seen him at the Midway golf driving range a few times. Admired his swing. She worked there part time. One of her favorite places to manhunt.

Paul Grim handed the inventory list to the two junior auditors. "Here, go get started. I'm using the men's room. I'll be out in a little while."

"Sure, boss. See you out there." They walked out the front door, across the lot and started the process.

"Let me show you the restroom, Paul. It is Paul, right?"

"Yeah, Laura. What makes me think you knew that?"

"Why, I have no idea. Here, it's right here." She held the door open and followed him in. He pushed her against a stall. "Squeeze my nipples…that's it…now spank me…hard!"

40

We Have Another Body

Corporal Creed called Bob into his office. "Close the door, Bob, have a seat."

Bob sat down on the hard wood chair. Office lore was the miserable chair was intentional—the Corporal didn't want anyone to get too comfortable. Bob looked across the immaculate old school metal desk. The Corporal was studying a file. Bob had been here before. It had never been comfortable.

"The Erik Stryker case, Bob. The young man you and Bobby identified. I need you to make an in-person notification to next of kin before it leaks and drops on social media."

Interesting, Bob thought. He would have bet the Corporal didn't know what social media was. And his use of "drops"? That term had to have come from his granddaughter. Furthermore, they hadn't made a positive identification. They'd found a paystub with a name on it. Bob couldn't understand how such an imbecile could work his way up to the rank of Corporal.

"You have any leads on parents or siblings, Bob?"

"Not yet. Visiting Club 654 this morning. Erik Stryker, the name on the paystub we found. He worked there. We'll find out more, get an address and family information hopefully. We'll make the notification."

"One more thing, Bob. I need you two to take the lead on this case. Homicide is swamped. They don't have the manpower right now."

"Sure, we're on it. We'll do some interviews." Bob thought he and Bobby could do a better job than homicide. That unit didn't like to get their shoes muddy. A waste of taxpayer money sometimes.

Bob left the building and called Bobby. He'd seen this many, many times in his career. Corporal Creed's comments about social media confirmed his view. The only thing management cared about was protecting the institution. It was the grunts who cared. About serving the people. "Bobby, I'm picking you up."

The scruffy, ponytailed bartender was washing glasses and looked up. Bob and Bobby sat down. Club 654 wasn't open for business. They must have climbed the back stairs from the restaurant below, he thought. He was prepping the club for the eight o'clock opening.

"Sorry guys, we aren't serving yet. I can get you some water if you like?" He'd said that before he turned and saw the uniforms. "Oh, how can I help you?"

Bob took out his compact recorder. " Sir, we'd like to ask you a few questions. Erik Stryker works here, right?"

"Yeah, he works here a few nights a week. He's a doorman." He didn't feel comfortable getting into a big discussion about Erik. They'd never got along. "You have any other questions, you should speak to the owner, Bo Thompson. He's here. In his office, around there. He pointed to the hallway at the end of the bar.

"Just one more question. Was Erik a bouncer?"

"No, no way. He just checked IDs and coats. That's all."

"Mr. Thompson. Good morning. We're with the Sheriff's office. Have a few questions about one of your employees. Have a minute?" Bob and Bobby had walked down the hall and located his office. Bob handed him his business card and flashed his ID.

"Sure, have a seat, fellas." Bo Thompson could breathe again. For a second he thought they were here for him.

"We understand Erik Stryker works for you. We're just looking to get his home address, that's all."

"Bo opened his desk file drawer and fingered through his employee files. "Here it is. Yeah, Erik Stryker. Here's the address. Anything else I can do for you? Everything OK? He didn't show up for work last night. Left early the night before. Said he was sick."

"Not right this minute. Thank you."

Bob and Bobby drove to Erik Stryker's house. It was a duplex in an area known for college student rentals. They would check out Erik's residence first in their quest for next of kin. The department secretary wasn't able to come up with anyone named Stryker anywhere close except Quinn Stryker. Quinn's address was the same as Erik's.

The house was an old wood framed duplex. The beige color was stained brown with splashed mud a few feet up from the cracked cinderblock foundation. There wasn't any grass to speak of. Puddles and trash led to the front door. Two dirty webbed folding chairs sat on the small porch. A white four door Jeep Rubicon was parked in front of the house. As they walked across the sidewalk, Bobby noticed the Jeep's tires were extremely muddy. Someone had been off-roading, he thought.

They knocked, then knocked several more times. Bob saw a curtain in a front window rustle. The door opened. "Hello officers. Something I can do for you?"

Bob showed his badge and asked if he was related to Erik Stryker.

"Yes, Erik is my brother. I'm Quinn Stryker."

"May we come in, Mr. Stryker? Bob noticed Quinn Stryker was glancing over his shoulder, as if someone was behind him.

"Sure, just let me get some pants on."

"I'm sorry to have to tell you this, Mr. Stryker. The body of a young man around your age was found last night. There was a paystub from Club 654 found with the body. It had your brother's name on it. Your brother worked there, we understand. We don't have a positive identification. We need you to come down to the morgue. See if it is Erik. That your Jeep out front? You can follow us."

Quinn's jaw dropped. "You think it's Erik? Oh…no…it can't

be. I need to change my clothes. I'll be right out."

While Bob had been talking, Bobby was looking around the room. Ignoring the piles of magazines stacked everywhere, he focused on a shelf on the wall leading to what he thought might be the kitchen. He spotted what appeared to be a family portrait among the knickknacks. He was about to move closer for a better look as Bob announced they were leaving.

As soon as they started the trip to the morgue, with Quinn following, the radio came to life. Dispatch announced, "Bob, Bobby, we have another body. A young woman. No need for action. Just FYI."

"That's number four, Bobby. If our dead boy is identified as Erik, his autopsy just got bumped."

41

Roses Are Red

They were all eerily alike. White. Blonde. Between eighteen and twenty-four. Five foot five to five foot seven. Weighed 125 to 135 pounds. Three women. Each found in rocky, wooded areas within the past two months. Discovered within a thirty mile radius. Nude, sexually assaulted and crudely covered with leaves and sticks. Cause of death was strangulation. The commonality didn't end there. Each crime victim exhibited two additional similarities. One rose had been placed in each victim's mouth. The roses were different colors—red, green and blue. The flowers were preserved with an acrylic sealer. And there were cryptic marks on their breasts. A circle four inches in diameter had been branded symmetrically. Inside the circles for the first victim the number "1" was found. The second woman had the number "2" singed inside the circles. And the number "3" was burned inside of victim three's circles.

Local law enforcement handled the initial investigation. When it became apparent that this was the handiwork of a serial killer, the homicide unit asked for assistance. Aligned under the FBI's critical incident response group, the National Center for the Analysis of Violent Crime was asked to assist. They conducted detailed analyses of crimes from different perspectives and offered advice as to how to investigate and apprehend violent offenders.

A fourth woman had just been found. She had a white rose placed in her mouth and the number "4" inside the circle branded on her breasts.

42

Conciliation

"**H**ey Jim. Sorry so long. You busy? I got a project at my friend's house I could use some help with. Can you come over?" Jo had suggested Jim might be able to help with the vault issue, so Candy reached out and made the call.

Jim pulled off to the shoulder so he could talk.

"Nice to hear from you, Candy. I have a meeting at my lawyer's office in a few minutes. Not sure how long it'll take. Text me the address."

When Candy said they needed a burner bar and someone to operate it, Jo had immediately thought that Jim Griot might be able to help. He sold to the heavy construction industry. She had heard that Jim worked for bridge demolition companies before he bought Essential Sales & Rental. He'd already met Candy. It'd be worth contacting him. She had no other ideas. Burner bars weren't listed for sale on Craigslist and people who knew how to use them weren't featured on LinkedIn.

Jim entered the law offices of Janice Barnes. He'd attended high school with her. They'd been good friends. Jim had helped protect her from bullying as best he could. Senior year he walked her to and from her car every day to make sure no one tormented her. She was one of a handful of lesbians in the entire school and was constantly subjected to unbelievable acts of cruelty. She was a top student and repaid him by tutoring. Janice got an academic scholarship to college and then graduated from Yale Law. She now had a dozen lawyers working for her, all women. She'd agreed to drive down from Nashville and meet him at one of her satellite locations.

"I wish we were meeting under more pleasant circumstances, Jim. It's so good to see you!"

"Same here, Janice. Haven't seen you since I bought my business. It's been too long. I'm really happy to see you've done so well. You deserve it. And I heard you got married. Congratulations. She better be treating you right."

"Thanks, Jim. She's treating me well. The alternative under the law wouldn't be pretty, would it?" Jim caught the upturned sliver of a smile.

"So, Jim, let's see what we have." Janice opened a manila file thick with paperwork. "They call it conciliation. That's the term the EEOC uses. A fancy term for 'work it out.' Negotiate an outcome that satisfies both parties. The EEOC will try to mediate a settlement before the issue goes to trial. This is the process that we want to participate in. In my opinion, if the EEOC investigates the complaint and considers it to be valid, they will suggest conciliation. That is what you and I want to happen, Jim. I have the charge notification from EEOC. It has a URL link to their respondent portal. I've accessed the charge already."

"You're a little ahead of me, Janice. Always were. Remember?"

"No worries. Here's my take. Jo Brooks filed a discrimination charge against Essential Sales & Rental. Jo Brooks claims she faced discrimination and harassment in the workplace. Do you dispute that? Do you have anyone who would support your claims if it went that far? Do you have any evidence to the contrary?"

"Well, let me think. First off, Jo Brooks was one of the best employees I've ever had. I was stunned when she resigned. If she says she was discriminated against and harassed, I believe it. She wouldn't have any reason to lie about it. My office manager, Laura Morningstar, had it in for Jo. I don't know what her problem is. Laura complained to me about Jo's work a bunch of times. Fact is, Jo was better at her job than Laura. Should never have hired Laura as a manager. Some people just can't get along with others. That's Laura. My guess is Laura is the one who discriminated against Jo.

She was Jo's immediate supervisor. She did the staff evaluations. I overheard the guys in the repair shop hassled Jo too. You know, catcalls and such. Never saw it happening, and nobody actually reported it to me directly. Jo was pretty thick skinned. I thought she could easily handle the guys. Wish Jo had come to me first. I paid Jo very well and was considering promoting her just before she left. I understand why she quit. Nobody should have to put up with that."

"OK, Jim here's my suggestion going forward. Let the EEOC conduct its preliminary investigation. If they find evidence of fact, we, and the other party, will receive a letter of determination. Then the EEOC will encourage us to settle. Mind you, they have six months to complete the investigation, so don't hold your breath. Be careful in the meantime. Don't talk about the complaint."

"I see, Janice. About the settlement amount. How much are we talking… on average?"

"Forty thousand, Jim. I want you to know that I know *you* had nothing to do with this complaint. I know better than anyone how fairly you treat people. Remember high school? We, as employers, can't control what our employees do to one another. We are required to act if we are aware of sexual harassment, discrimination and so forth. Obviously you weren't aware. I'm waiving my fee on this one, Jim."

Jim sat in the parking lot. He added up the dollar amounts. The meetings he attended today resulted in a total amount owed of three hundred sixty thousand dollars.

He texted Candy.

"Hey. Just finished up here. Got your address. I'll text you when I have time to visit."

43

Mommy Dearest

Laura Morningstar had been the office manager at Essential Sales & Rental for several years. Jim Griot hired her through an employment agency. Her resume indicated she had extensive general office experience. It was soon discovered she had experience in other areas.

Laura pulled her skirt down and turned to face him. "That was nice, Paul. Good job." The chief auditor at Bank Two and the office manager finished dressing and exited the men's room. Laura wasn't going to be able to sit for a while. They'd met at the local golf driving range six months ago. Laura pursued him aggressively. He was just another one of the many men she used for sexual gratification. In her mid-forties, she attracted males from sixteen to sixty years old. Petite, pretty, fit, approachable and agreeable, she let men know she was available, and then taught them how she liked it.

Laura's teen years had been troubled. A contractor working at her parents' home got her pregnant when she was fifteen. Her parents insisted she have an abortion. She struggled at school until her parents enlisted a tutor to help her in math and another for science. The only tutors available at the time were male. Within days she was sleeping with both. At eighteen she was once again pregnant. This time she handled the abortion arrangements herself.

Laura enrolled at the local community college after graduating high school and studied business and accounting part time. She'd moved out and had a full-time job working for a large construction supplies distributor. The owner quickly promoted her. She was now his personal assistant. He was ten years older and had three-year-old boys, identical twins. His wife had died two years ago. He told Laura that his deceased wife was an alcoholic and a terrible mother. The twins suffered while she was alive. The fatal car accident had been a blessing of sorts, he said.

It started innocently. Laura was asked to watch the twins after work Monday through Friday from four to six. Their full time nanny went home at four. They were enrolled in preschool three days a week—three hours per day. Laura loved working with them on motor skills, numbers, letters and especially colors. She set up an activity board and they practiced matching shapes and colors. She used colored pipe cleaners and a colander and showed them how to thread the cleaners through the holes, connect them and make shapes.

Her boss would come home with takeout for everyone most nights and they'd have dinner together. Within a few weeks, she was having torrid sex with him, just as she'd planned. This time, however, it would be much harder to move on to another partner.

Her boss, Greg Waller, was an abusive freak. Laura was surprised when, after a month, he asked her to perform oral on him in front of the twins. He insisted that she squeal when he came on her face, letting it ooze down and off her chin. She was reluctant at first, but agreed. She thought the boys were young enough. They'd have no memory of it. Greg set up a camera. Then it was her turn to receive. After bringing her close with his mouth, he'd finish her up with two fingers fast and hard. The twins were wide eyed, curious and timidly tried to touch at first. Greg encouraged that. The nightly encounters progressed to mutual fondling. Laura was told to fellate them when they had the uneventful erections most toddlers experienced. The boys were taught to simulate breastfeeding. Greg made sure they were synchronized in their efforts. By the next year, when they turned four, Greg had taught them how to bring Laura to orgasm digitally and orally. The sessions almost always ended in tears and tantrums. The twins no longer wanted anything to do with the games they were being forced to play. Ice cream and brownies along with Laura' steady voice helped soothe them.

Laura couldn't explain why she didn't end the relationship with Greg and his twins. She'd never stayed with anyone that long. The addition of the twins to her sex life with Greg was so erotic, she thought that was the reason she stayed involved until they turned six. Three mouths, three pairs of hands, and one large penis satisfying her simultaneously wasn't easy to abandon. Greg had decided to sell the business by then anyway. It was time for Laura to find a new job and new playmates.

She'd managed to finish college by the time she was twenty-four, and worked for several industrial distributors before joining Essential Sales & Rental. She was forty-five now. She looked thirty. Laura had retained her innate ability to attract men and her inclination to discard them quickly.

44

Who's That Girl?

When his shift concluded at Double Donuts, Quinn Stryker elected to take a detour before going home. He'd shared the Jeep with his brother. They'd split the expenses incurred. Sometimes they would flip a coin to see who could use it when they both needed transportation the same day or night. The loser used their Uber app. The Jeep was his alone now. His brother was refrigerated in the morgue.

It was late afternoon when Quinn drifted into the parking space at Essential Sales & Rental. He'd driven up and down the lot looking for the F-250 he'd captured on his phone. It wasn't there. Quinn sauntered into the lobby. A sharply dressed blonde woman rounded the corner.

"May I help you?" Laura Morningstar ruled the entrance area with passion. She made sure no visitors were admitted without an appointment. Her receptionist was on break.

"Maybe. Hi, I'm Quinn. I am looking for a woman." He pulled a red scarf out of his pocket. He'd fished it out of a bag of clothes in the Jeep. "I saw her drop this where I work and wanted to return it. I think she might work here. She drives a red Mazda Miata? Blonde hair? You know her?"

Laura thought she recognized the young man. She couldn't place him, but was positive she'd seen him before. He was very cute, she thought. He impressed her as being shy and innocent. His hands were shaking.

"Why yes, I know who you are talking about. Jo Brooks. She doesn't work here anymore though. I'm not sure where she went. Someone told me she's working at the Triple Z on 43. You might try there. If I can help you more, just stop by, anytime, Quinn.

Nice to meet you."

"Thank you…um…." She was older but she definitely had the physical characteristics that aroused him. He felt like he knew her the second she appeared before him.

"It's Laura, Quinn. Laura Morningstar."

He knew Laura's name and where she worked. And she was perfect. *When?*

Quinn was in no hurry to return to his house. Without Erik things weren't the same. He couldn't shake the image of Erik's contorted face. The face he'd identified as his brother at the morgue. The officers who led him to the morgue didn't go in with him as the attendant lifted the sheet. Erik's face was bloated, cut, and bruised, as if he'd been beaten and dragged. He was barely recognizable.

Quinn parked across the street. The Triple Z diner was in full view. He'd been sitting, watching, for hours. Then he saw it. A red Miata was parking in one of the spaces designated for employees. The driver checked her makeup in the rearview mirror and tossed her scarf over her shoulder. When she swung her leg wide to get out, he enjoyed a flash of silver panties. His eyes followed her short black skirt up the stairs and she disappeared inside.

He knew Jo's name and where she worked. And she was perfect. *When?*

45

Burner Bars And Fast Cars

"Mornin', Candy. Stopping at Double Donuts and then I'll be at your place by six."

"Great, Jim! Mornin' to you. Could you pick up two strawberry sprinkled donuts and a medium hot coffee with cream, sugar, and caramel?"

"Sure. See you in a few."

Candy hadn't thought about that breakfast order in years. A former client who would visit early three times a week was trained to bring her those treats. He'd also bring a pack of Newport 100's, a few condoms, and three hundred dollars.

Jim walked in carrying her order and Candy led him to her commercial grade chef's kitchen. Jim stopped and stared at her forty-six-inch Thor range. She hadn't turned it on more than twice since she'd moved in. She was surprised he hadn't said a word about the house or grounds. Surprised and relieved. She wasn't comfortable with all the compliments.

"I think you know each other, Jim." Jo was sitting at the quartz topped island.

"Yeah, we do! Hey, Jo. What's it, twice in a few weeks?" He wasn't going to ask what Jo was doing here. He didn't even know why he was invited. He was grateful his trusty Valium had kicked in.

"Yeah, so it is. This time you brought *us* donuts." Jo smiled warmly.

Candy handed Jo a strawberry sprinkle. "Jim, first I wanna thank you for coming so early. Might not be early for you, but it definitely is for me. We're in a situation and running out of time. Jo thought you might be able to help. Or if not, point us in the right direction."

Jim couldn't help wonder if this had something to do with the EEOC complaint. "Well, I'll do my best."

"OK, here's our problem. Please don't judge. I don't know if you remember. At Club 654 I told you I was staying at a friend's house?"

"Yes, of course. I remember."

"So, this here is my friend's house. But it's his *and* mine. We aren't married or anything but we own it together. I met Jo at the club the same night I met you. We've been hanging out ever since. The reason I asked you here today is we're in trouble. You see, there's a vault here, down underground. The combination is lost. We need to get it open soon. Jo thought you might be able to help."

"Ahh…sounds like quite the problem. Is your friend here? The friend you own the house with? Are all three of you in trouble?"

Jo had told Candy that Jim was not only handsome and nice, but extremely smart. He wouldn't try to open a safe at a house whose ownership was sketchy.

"He's not home now and, yeah, all three of us are in some shit. Look, he doesn't know you're here. It's OK. We have a job you might be able to do. If you can handle it, he, er…his name is Scorp, will be happier than any of us. If you take the job, he'll be here when you do it. I'm not scammin' you. I promise."

"OK, OK, enough foreplay." Jim held his arms up in surrender. "Let's take a look." They took the elevator to sub level one.

"Well, here it is. All new, shiny and locked." Candy swiped her hand across the front of the vault.

"Hmm…you know how thick it is?"

"Three inches. It's special concrete and stainless steel. Scorp, my friend, says you need a burner bar to get in. Is that right, Jim?"

"Yes. There isn't any material on earth it can't cut. What's inside?"

"Money, guns, and ammunition." Candy made no mention of the drugs.

"That's a problem. The bar will get up to 8000 degrees. It'll burn right through the door pretty quick. The bills and the ammunition might not survive."

"We have to try, Jim. Whatever happens, happens. Can you get one of them and use it?"

"Yeah, I actually have one at the shop. I used it when I was doing bridge demolition. It's like a giant sparkler once you light it off. What's that door down the hall on the right go to, Candy?"

"That's a tool room."

"It's far enough away. Shouldn't be an issue. I need to get into the mechanical room though. It's near the vault. Could present a problem."

"I've never opened either door, Jim. Can that wait? Will you do the job for us?

"Well, I feel like I should have you and your friend sign something. You know, so I'm not legally responsible for what happens."

"Would a million cash convince you to try? And I'll throw in a hot Challenger SRT8."

"And I'll drop the EEOC complaint, Jim." Jo crossed her heart.

46

Dental Solution

"Dr. Haspert? Kate Finder here. Would you have a few minutes to chat? I'm a local private investigator. My clients have retained me in a missing person case. I just have a few simple questions."

David Haspert was delighted. Since his new cosmetic procedure had gone viral, he'd stopped answering most phone calls and emails. Something different and easy, he thought.

"I'd be happy to help, Ms. Finder."

"Great! My clients are a local couple trying to locate a young woman and her child who'd been living with them in Annapolis. The issue is they do not know her last name. Apparently they were given a false name. The couple indicated that you lived across the street from them with this woman and another woman. Her first name is Gina and the second woman goes by Candy. Gina has a three-year-old. A girl. Her name is Lily. My goal is to find out the last names of these two women, so I may locate Gina for my client."

Just hearing Candy and Gina's names energized David. Remember them? That was the understatement of the millennium. The year and a half he spent with them were the happiest years of his life. He'd been going through a rough patch professionally and emotionally when he met them. He was a changed man when he left them. He could almost smell them on his fingers.

"Her name is Gina Lamartina. Her friend is Candise Doubleday. Candy's boyfriend's name is Scorp. Just Scorp. Her father's name was Manic. He was a UFC fighter at one time. He's deceased. I know nothing about Gina's parents. Candy and Scorp were in the process of having a house built in Tennessee the last I heard. Oh, and they were all New Jersey residents prior to moving here. That's all I can share with you. Sorry."

"That's all I need, Dr. Haspert. Thank you very much. I'll let you return to your busy day."

The private investigator called Audrey Abrams. "You are looking for Gina Lamartina. Her friend is Candise Doubleday. Would you like me to go further?"

"That's a great start. Thank you. Yes, please see what other details you can find. Like we said, we are sure Gina went to the Nashville area." Audrey winked at Syd.

"OK, Mrs. Abrams. Knowing a last name and Nashville won't be nearly enough to find her. I will attempt to utilize any records I can find for either of them. I'll need some time and an increase to my retainer."

"Whatever it takes, Ms. Finder, whatever it takes." Audrey was tenacious when she wanted something.

David Haspert hung up as he sat at his massive mahogany desk, drumming his pencil on a notepad. He had it all, he thought. The respect of the dental community. A patented cosmetic dental procedure that would continue to enrich him throughout his lifetime. A private waterfront estate as well as a share in a corporate jet. Even with all that he had accomplished, he felt, once again, that something was missing. Perhaps a new facility near Nashville might help him fill the void?

47

Surrounded By Turkeys

"**Y**ou know, they don't give them much, Bobby." Bob and Bobby were on their way to Mountaintop Medical Center. They had to initiate an interview with the brothers they'd arrested to see if they had anything to do with Erik Stryker's death. Sam and Dave had been sent to the county detention center initially to await their court appearance for possession of methamphetamine. Their health had deteriorated rapidly. They were transferred to Mountain View. "Yeah, I know, Bob. Think they just get something for blood pressure control in lockup."

The two policemen checked in and located the room. Sam and Dave were in the same semi-private room. Their nurse motioned them to join her outside.

"I understand you need to question them, but I'm sure they won't be much help to you. They were severely dehydrated on arrival. Delusional. They've been hydrated, sedated, and restrained. Their blood tests just came back from the lab. They both have liver and kidney damage. There are signs of malnutrition. We've scheduled a time to extract all their remaining teeth. They are rotted and will cause ongoing infections throughout their systems. To add to this, they both tested positive for hepatitis and HIV. Approximately twenty percent of meth cases this far advanced never recover mentally…ever."

"Thank you for the recap. We just have to follow up with them. It's a damn shame. They aren't that old. Certainly not as old as they look. Let's get started, Bob."

Only Sam was awake. Dave was motionless, breathing through his mouth. Spittle mixed with blood was oozing out his mouth onto his pillow.

"Sir! Hello! Can you hear me?" Bobby took the lead. Sam's eyes were open but Bobby wasn't sure he could see as he was rolling them around.

"Remember where you live? Who you live with? Who you cook with?"

Sam closed his eyes. "Trailer, Tracy Lynne, big tits, party, Candy, chickens, spiders." His voice trailed off as he tried to answer. Unresponsive.

"That went well, Bob. I wasn't expecting to get anything out of them two."

"Yeah, we have a name and a description. Well, sort of a description. Think we can eliminate the spiders and chickens as suspects. It's time to visit the trailer."

Tracy Lynne didn't know where Sam and Dave were. It wasn't that unusual for them to wander off for days or weeks at a time. She was extremely disappointed that Candy had flaked out on her. She'd even stopped hitting the meth in anticipation. She'd decided to stay at their place until her friends returned. She had nothing better to do. She was watching The Price is Right when the knock on the trailer door startled her.

"Hello, officers. How may I help you?" Tracy Lynne was wearing her favorite mustard stained wife-beater tee shirt and a pair of torn leggings. She held the battered door open and was leaning out.

"We'd like to ask you a few questions, ma'am, if that's alright. I'm Bobby and this here's Bob."

"Bout what?" Tracy hadn't been high for days. She wasn't concerned.

"About the dead boy found up behind the store up there. You knew about that?"

"Yeah, heard about it. Don't know nothing about it though."

"Please step out ma'am. What's your name?"

"OK, I'm coming. Name's Tracy Lynne. Just staying here. This

146

ain't my trailer."

Bobby kicked a few plastic one-liter bottles. "Well, guess it's a good thing you don't live here. Somebody's been cooking meth here. You know who that might be? Maybe Sam and Dave?"

"Maybe, officers. Really don't know. This is their trailer, though. Haven't seen them for a while. Not sure where they are."

"Oh, we know where they are. They're in jail." Bobby took his notepad out.

"They mentioned your name when we interviewed them. Any reason they'd mention you? And they mentioned something about big tits and candy. You know why they would talk about that? Bobby took his pen out as if he was ready to take notes. He'd found this to be helpful before. It made the person being interviewed feel important.

Tracy Lynne shook her head. "They said my name because we're good friends and I hang out with them a lot down here. They weren't talkin' about candy like you eat. Was talkin' bout a *girl* we met named Candy. She has double Ds for sure. Has an accent like Tony Soprano, you know, like some Jersey girl."

"Does Candy hang out here?" Bob scribbled on his notepad.

"She did once. The day…or maybe the day before that dead boy was found. She was supposed to come back and party with Sam, Dave, and me. She flaked on us. Disappeared. Won't answer my calls."

"Anything else you can tell us about this Candy person, Tracy Lynne?" Bob glanced at Bobby.

"She was a pretty little thing. Built nice, blonde hair and she drove a purple Challenger with shiny black wheels. She had a backpack full of hundred dollar bills with her."

"Would you happen to have her phone number?"

"Sure, it's in my phone. Here."

They noted the phone number for Candy and asked for Tracy Lynne's number too.

"That's all the questions we have for now. We'll call if anything else comes up."

Bob and Bobby turned to leave. "Oh, and one more thing. You need to clean up their yard. Enough chemicals here to kill a herd of elephants. Sam and Dave won't be coming home for quite some time."

As they were getting into their unmarked car, Bobby commented. "You know Bob, the way this case has gone so far reminds me just how hard it is to soar with the eagles when you're surrounded by freakin' turkeys."

48

Road Service

Why not *now*? Quinn waited through an entire shift change at the diner. He noticed a few employees come out, start their cars and leave. It was time. He drove the Jeep a mile down the road in the direction she'd come from. There was a little pull-off with a picnic table and a grill that sat on a pole cemented into the ground. Enough room for several cars. He backed up, pulled off to the side of the road, got out and raised the hood on the Jeep and waited. Several cars slowed down as they neared. He waved them off. Then he saw it. The red Miata. Quinn stood in the middle of the road waving his arms madly. The Miata slowed to a crawl and then stopped.

Jo put the window down. She knew what it felt like to be stranded. "Broke down?"

"Yeah, thanks for stopping. Left my phone home. Could you call road service for me?"

He looked exactly like Erik Stryker. Jo froze. Quinn reached in, yanked her toward the door and pushed the Vipertek stun gun against her neck. Three seconds later she was dazed and unable to move. Quinn dragged her out of the Miata and stuffed her limp body her into the Jeep's back seat. He gathered her phone, keys, and wallet. After moving the Miata between the grill and the picnic table, he locked it then put the hood down on the Jeep and sped away. He turned off Highway 43 into Dolly's Self-service Carwash. He chose the deluxe wash. As the Jeep creeped through, Quinn hopped into the back seat, gagged Jo and injected her with three milligrams of midazolam.

With the Jeep nice and clean, Quinn drove home. After driving around the block, he backed up to the rear of his side of the duplex house. Within a minute he'd dragged Jo down the basement steps. After unlocking the door, he pulled Jo across the floor and up onto a mattress. Before he turned in for the night, he shot her up with an additional dose of the sedative.

Quinn woke up very early, before sunrise. He picked up a syringe and listened at the top of the basement stairs. All quiet. He descended to the basement. Jo was in the same position as he had left her. A new dose was ready and he eagerly plunged the needle into her arm. His heartrate was rising fast. His hands were shaking and sweating as he removed her diner uniform top. He reached around, unhooked her bra and leaned down and sucked, moving from one breast to the other. He reached down and felt his arousal. He stroked her thigh and fingered her belly button jewelry. The pictures push-pinned low on the basement wall next to her caught his eye. Now, he knew. This could wait. He dressed and hurried out to the Jeep. This would be the best day of his life.

Laura Morningstar checked her email while she sipped her morning tea. She couldn't stop daydreaming about Quinn, the young man she'd talked to at the office. The handsome guy who was looking for Jo Brooks. Jo Brooks? What did he see in *her*? I would show him what a mature, experienced woman could do, she thought. There was something about him. Maybe it was his eyes? His lips? She'd have to get closer and find out.

It was early. Laura loved going in to work early. It was quiet and she could relax without phones or interruption. As she drove down the narrow side road leading to the equipment yard, there was a white Jeep with its hood up. As she drew closer, she saw him. It was Quinn, waving her down. Work might have to wait, or not happen at all today, she thought.

It had been bothering him since the second he met her. Laura Morningstar. The petite, pretty woman at Essential Sales & Rental was so familiar. The way she walked and talked, as well as her features, reminded him of someone. This morning, when he looked at the pictures pinned to his basement wall just above the mattress Jo was lying on, it struck him, hard. There was Laura Morningstar, many years younger, naked. Erik and he were attached to her breasts and their little hands were exploring. Their father was standing over her, jamming it down her throat. Their father had inked *Three Musketeers* at the bottom of the polaroid.

"Hi, Quinn! Hey, need some help?" Laura pulled her Camry in front of the Jeep. She hiked up her skirt to near panty level and adjusted her jacket zipper. Substantiated confidence.

Quinn was an expert. He'd practiced ten minutes a day, every day. The process of releasing the safety on his stun gun, holding the charge button down, and pressing it against his prey for exactly three to five seconds perfected. He walked up to Laura's car, greeted her with a wide smile, and rendered her helpless before she realized what was happening. He secured her purse and phone and threw them, along with her limp body into his Jeep. The trees and shrubs lining the road screened his actions from the main road. Her took advantage of that and gagged and drugged Laura. She was a feisty one, he thought. She'd started rolling her head side to side as he started to tie the rubber tubing gag. The midazolam injection ensured she would be perfectly still during the trip to his house. She would soon join Jo Brooks. He was elated. This woman would pay dearly for her part in destruction of their childhood innocence. As he moved her into the basement, he thought about his twin brother Erik. How proud he would be.

Laura could see the picture. Quinn had placed her next to Jo on the ratty mattress in his basement and propped her head up slightly, facing the wall. He wanted her to see what she had done to Erik and himself. Laura squinted in the dim light. Now she knew why his face was so familiar. She was groggy and her muscles didn't react to her brain's request for movement. She felt a hand on her shoulder. Quinn rolled her over. Her clothes were missing and she felt a slight chill. The sound and smell preceded the pain by a second. Her gag-muffled scream couldn't be heard. He was kneeling over her. She could see the red hot metal circle at the end of a rod that he was holding. Some of her flesh was stuck to it and a wisp of smoke jumped off and filled the air. She gritted her teeth against the gag as she saw him move it over and down onto her other breast. Her body arched in reaction as he pushed a second hot iron inside each circle. He threw the branding irons aside. His hands encircled her neck. He entered her as she gasped and took her last breaths.

Before he left for work, Quinn upped the dosage of sedative and medicated Jo properly. She would remain calm until he returned.

49

It's Complicated

"Let's go, Jamey. Find a motel closer to Scorp's place and set up base there." Abe had lost any semblance of patience. This was just taking too much time and Gina and her kid were slowing them down. Drying their hair took forever. Then there was the nail polish and makeup. Ridiculous.

Jamey visited Gina and Lily before they checked out. Abe was busy on his burner trying to reach his contact at the Port of Wilmington. He wanted to know when the stolen cars were scheduled to be loaded and shipped. He was told it was too late to interrupt the process. He'd hoped he could somehow stop the shipment. Abe's phone call afforded Jamey a private moment.

"Good morning ladies." Lily ran over and jumped up into his arms. She liked him. He tickled her, played with her, and was nice to her mom. Nicer than the old man they used to live with. Jamey sat down on one of the beds. Gina joined him. "You sneak off? Abe getting to you already this morning?"

"I can't put up with him too much longer, Gina. You know, I never spent this much time at once with him. He's always been high strung and now the money problem has made him crazy. Let's talk about something more pleasant, while we can."

Gina was so curious. This guy she'd known for such a short time, who knew so little about her and her past, was suddenly becoming the man she'd always dreamed of. He didn't want anything from her. He wasn't taking advantage of her. He didn't look at her like a starved animal. "You know I'm due pretty soon, Jamey. I'm going to see if Scorp and Candy will let me stay with them, until I can, like, get a job and an apartment. I'm not sure about Scorp. I mean, he always treated me well and we had some good times, the three of us. Before they left Annapolis I knew I wasn't gonna be included in their future. That's how I ended up with Syd and Audrey. You know, near where you guys first met me. It was OK there for a while, but there was stuff goin' on in that house I didn't want Lily to know about."

Jamey wanted to ask who Lily's father was and if he was still in their life. Was he also the father of the baby she was about to have? He wanted to know if it would affect what he hoped would be his future.

"I'm sure you'll figure it all out soon, Gina. We'll both find an answer to our problems."

A knock at the door interrupted their conversation. "Jamey! Let's go. Now!"

After driving closer to Scorp's house, Abe saw a sign. "This will do." They checked into the Streamside Inn.

50

Voicemail

Candy threw herself down on her bed in frustration. Jo wasn't answering her calls. She'd always picked up. Jo was late. She was never late. They'd arranged to meet with Jim at the house to finalize plans. Jim was dropping off the burner bar and the other equipment needed for the job. Once everything was in place, Candy would call Scorp, tell him what was about to happen, and ask him to come over to put his stamp of approval on the operation. There was no way Scorp would object, she thought.

Another two hours passed. Jim was now late. Candy had called and texted him a dozen times. He wasn't picking up or answering. What was going on?

Candy was bedside herself. They were so close to solving the puzzle. She thought she might drive over to Essential Sales & Rental, but what if Jim was already on his way and arrived while she was out? He'd just have to wait if that happened. She googled the name of the diner were Jo mentioned she'd been working, the Triple Z.

"Triple Z diner, Jasmine speaking. How may I help you?"

"Hi ma'am, my name's Candise. I'm a friend of Jo's. I've been trying to reach her. I apologize for calling her at work, but she hasn't answered any of my calls and that is very unusual. Is she there?"

"No, I'm sorry. She isn't here. She didn't show up for work this morning. The boss called her and it went to voicemail."

"Oh, I see, thank you."

"Oh…and one of the cooks told me he thought he saw her car parked at a picnic spot up the road a little. Maybe her car broke down."

"OK, thanks. If she comes in, tell her Candy called."

Candy Googled Essential Sales & Rental, then punched in their phone number. "Hello, may I please speak with Jim Griot. I'm calling about a rental I'm expecting to arrive today."

"May I ask who's calling?"

"Oh, I'm a friend. Name's Candy. Jim was supposed to lend my husband some sort of tool. Said he'd drop it off this morning. I've tried Jim's cell but he hasn't answered. Went to voicemail."

"I'm sorry. Mr. Griot hasn't been in this morning. Let me connect you with our office manager, Laura Morningstar. Please hold."

After a few minutes the receptionist reconnected with Candy. "I'm very sorry, ma'am. Ms. Morningstar isn't in either. I've called both of them on their cells and got voicemail. Could I leave a message, or would you like to leave a voicemail here for Mr. Griot?"

"No, that's OK. I appreciate your help."

Candy called Khloe. "Hey, Khloe. It's Candy. Why doesn't your boyfriend buy a fuckin' phone? Put him on."

"Your girlfriend wants to talk to you, Scorp. I'll be outside." She tossed the phone to Scorp.

"Hey, what's up? Find out anything yet about a burner bar?"

"Yeah, I did, with Jo's help. Found a guy who has one. He knows how to use it and he's willing to help. For a million in cash and my car."

"So, what are we waiting for. Let's do it."

"He was supposed to be here earlier today. Then we were gonna call you to come over. He didn't show up, isn't answering his phone, and neither is Jo."

Jim's lawyer, Janice Barnes, specialized in white collar crime. It was widespread, fairly easy to defend, and lucrative. She'd helped Jim as a friend with the necessary contract work when he bought his business. Now she was assisting with his EEOC predicament. She had just returned from lunch when the call came in to her direct line.

"Ms. Barnes?"

"Yes, this is Janice Barnes."

"I have a collect call from the Grand Valley Detention Center. Will you accept the charges?"

"Yes, of course."

"Janice? It's Jim. I've been arrested .I need help. Can you help me? Get me out of here?"

"Don't say anything else, Jim. I'm on my way."

"OK, OK. Thank you so much. I was praying I wouldn't get voicemail."

51

Observation Eavesdrop

Bobby was on vacation. He wouldn't be back to work for three weeks. The Erik Stryker investigation would continue without him. Bob called the number Tracy Lynne gave them for the woman she called Candy. The number wasn't valid. Bob knew it could be a burner phone or a burner app used on an Android or iPhone. It could possibly be traced by going to the providers. He wasn't willing to jump through the required hoops. Tracy wasn't even sure what day the call was made. If it were a more important case he'd make the requisition.

Bob retraced his steps. The new information provided by Tracy Lynne led him back to Club 654. He had additional questions for the bartender and owner.

"Good morning, officer. See you are back. How may I be of service today?" Club 654's bartender was wiping down the expansive bar. He finished and launched the rag into a bin, turned, and bowed. Bob didn't care for the attitude. He'd try to make this brief but uncomfortable.

"Last time I was here I asked you about Erik Stryker. We found his body face down in the mud about fifty miles from here. He'd been clocked real good with a hard object. So, right now, I need your un-fuckin'-divided attention. Got it? The last night he worked here, did you see him with a little blonde? She would've been well endowed. Maybe new in town. Possibly a New York, New Jersey accent?"

"Hmm…let me see. Yeah, there was a woman I'd never seen before in here that night. Didn't pay much attention to her looks. She was little, I think. Wasn't here all night. Had a few drinks. She was talking to Jim Griot. He's in here a lot. He owns Essential Sales or something like that. She was chattin' him up. She definitely had a Jersey accent. He left and she left right after that. I remember because she gave me a brand new fifty dollar bill and told me to keep the change. That never happens here."

"So, you didn't see her talk to anyone else, or leave with anyone?"

"Not that I recall, officer. Maybe Bo saw more. He can see what's going on outside on the street from his office. You might want to check with him. Anything else I can help you with?"

"Not now."

Bob walked down the hall to Bo Thompson's office. "Mr. Thompson. I need to ask some additional questions about Erik Stryker. We found him with his head crushed lying in in a mud puddle. It was a long ways from here."

"Oh, no, that's awful! He wasn't a bad kid, you know. That's a damn shame."

"Regarding the night Erik went home sick. I have a question. Do you know if he left with anyone? Possibly a friend or someone he met here that night?"

"Well, yeah, maybe." Bo stood up and walked closer to his large office window that overlooked the street in front of Club 654. The view extended for several blocks in either direction. "I can see a lot from here. I remember seeing Erik walking arm in arm with two women that night, right after he told me he was sick and asked if he could leave. I wasn't pissed or anything. In fact, I was happy for the boy. He was always so shy and withdrawn. It was nice to see him with them. They got in a beige or tan minivan. Looked brand new."

"Do you know who the women were, Mr. Thompson? Maybe they were regulars here?"

"Well, I can't be positive, but one of the women was familiar. She had a red scarf around her neck. Looked like Jo Brooks. She's always got a red scarf on, whether it's hot or cold. She's kind of a regular. I guess you'd say that. Works at Jim Griot's place. I've seen her leave with women before. I think, she is, er…you know."

"No, I don't know. Tell me, Mr. Thompson."

"Jo is a lesbian."

"And the woman walking with Erik and Jo Brooks?"

"A short blonde. Never seen her before."

Bob parked his unmarked Explorer at the entrance. He walked into Essential Sales & Rental. There wasn't a soul manning the reception desk. He sat down and fidgeted, waiting for someone to appear. After a few minutes, an older woman turned the corner.

"Oh, sorry officer, we're a bit shorthanded today. Hope you weren't waiting long."

"Not a problem ma'am. Needed a rest. I'm here on official business." Bob liked the sound of that. "I'd like to speak with Jim Griot."

"I'm afraid that isn't possible. He didn't come in today and we haven't been able to reach him."

"I see. Well, I also need to speak with Jo Brooks."

"Oh my, I'm sorry. She no longer works here."

"Do you have an address for her? Maybe you know where she is employed now?"

"I heard she works at the Triple Z diner. You'd have to speak to human resources to get her home address. Our HR director is at a seminar this week."

"Could I speak with Ms. Brooks' supervisor? You know, her boss, when she was employed here?"

"Unfortunately, her supervisor, Ms. Morningstar, didn't come in today as well. We haven't been able to reach her. I saw her car on the side of the entrance road on my way in, but she isn't here. I'm sorry, I haven't been much help. If you stop back another day I'm sure we could answer your questions."

Bob left and stopped at Double Donuts for a coffee and some honey dips. Sitting in his truck, he reviewed his notes and listened to the recordings of all the interviews that had been completed to date. He wished Bobby had delayed his vacation. It would be nice to have a second set of eyes and ears on this one. He made a note: Jo–Candy–Erik–Purple Challenger–Beige Minivan. When he looked up, he saw Quinn Stryker walk out of the shop and empty the outside trashcans. Bob didn't know Quinn worked there. Probably because he usually used the drive-thru, he thought.

52

Labor Intensive

Abe checked in for them. The Streamside Inn was more luxurious than Brown's motel. The plastic cups in their rooms were actually sealed to protect them. And the TV worked.

"We need to get to Scorp's house, Jamey. I'm sick of this. It's taking too long. Gina can drop us and the kid off somewhere near Scorp's place. She can go and visit Scorp and Candy by herself like we planned, and report back to us. Let's go!"

Lily was complaining. "We just got here, mommy. Do we have to get back in the truck?"

Jamey winked at her. "I'll play a game with you on the way, Lily." Gina smiled. Jamey stepping up was nice, she thought.

Abe was driving. He was tapping the steering wheel nervously. Jamey was checking out the scenery. Now he understood why they were called the Smoky Mountains. They were driving in and out of low, wispy clouds that traveled across the road ahead. Lily was asleep.

"Guys…guys…my water broke!" Gina reached and put her hand on Jamey's shoulder. "I need to get to a hospital…quick."

"What! You're having a baby right here? Now? What the…." Abe was freaking out. He knew zero about babies, pregnancy, or anything else concerning women. "You're gonna have to hold off, Gina. We got work to do."

"Abe, it doesn't work like that. No such thing as holding off. Gina, how many weeks are you?" Jamey turned slightly and held her hand.

"Thirty-five weeks, maybe thirty-six. I have to get to a hospital…now."

"Yeah, OK, we'll get you there. Pull over, Abe. I'll set the navigation."

"You can't be serious. We're almost there. Can't this wait?"

"No, Abe, it can't wait. Gina needs to be in the hospital. The baby's life could depend on it."

"You haven't had any contractions, have you, Gina?"

"No. When I had Lily I had them before my water broke."

"Mommy, are you OK? What happened?"

"Mommy's OK. Your little sister will be here pretty soon."

"Hopefully you'll start in a day or so. The important thing is that you both are safe. We're about forty minutes away from Mountain View Hospital. Here, Lily, scooch up on my lap. Give your mom some room."

He'd once again surprised her, Gina thought. Jamey knew something about water breaking, contractions, and childbirth. Amazing.

Jamey took Gina by the arm and Lily by the hand and walked them into the emergency room at Mountain View Hospital. Abe complained about the detour vehemently. He couldn't understand why Jamey was catering to Gina and Lily. He vowed he would never, ever, work with him again. He was angry that he'd agreed to bring them along. He had to think. This was getting off track and out of control.

Jamey kept Lily occupied in the waiting room. Gina had been admitted quickly, he thought. Nothing like the big city hospitals he was used to. He wasn't allowed in to see her. He'd have to keep checking back. He took Lily into the cafeteria and they had a late lunch together. She had some questions about where mommy was and what was wrong with her. He tried his best to reassure her.

They finished lunch and were playing a game on his phone when the text came in

You're on your own bro. I'm gonna take care of this all by myself.

Jamey had no intention of answering Abe. He had more important business at hand.

Abe sighed. He was finally there. Sitting outside the gated property, he opened a bottle of Makers Mark bourbon. He'd been saving it to celebrate when they got paid. He took a long, slow draw. Scorp's house was nice enough, he thought. He'd take it in place of payment for sure. He put the Expedition in four-wheel drive low, and the brush bar on the front of the big SUV crushed the six foot aluminum fence with ease. He sped up close to the front door and stopped. With the Glock 19 machine pistol in one hand and the Browning automatic twelve gauge shotgun in the other, he walked up to the front door. He held the Browning up high and away from the house and fired. The blast shook the first floor windows. He waited for the echoes to subside, then rang the doorbell.

Candy jumped awake. She'd spent the day trying to contact Jim and Jo and had fallen asleep in the family room recliner. The gunshot that woke her up must have been right outside. Then she heard the doorbell. She looked out the front window. An eight-foot section of the security fence was flattened. There was a big SUV in front of the house. A bearded man was standing on the landing at the top of the front steps. He was holding a shotgun and some sort of pistol.

53

Teletracking

Kate Finder went to work. Armed with the last names she'd gleaned from Dr. David Haspert and the fact that Gina Lamartina was eight or more months pregnant and headed to the Nashville area, she rounded up her team. She divided up the lists. There were one hundred seventy-five hospitals in Tennessee. Twenty-eight were government hospitals and seventy-six were private. The instructions: call every hospital on your list four times a day and ask if a Gina Lamartina is a patient. Unless she has requested that her name not be released, the hospital will answer the question.

"Kate, I found Gina Lamartina. She's been admitted to Mountain View Hospital. Not too far from Great Smoky Mountain State Park." One of Kate Finder's interns broke the news.

"Great work. Thank you!" Kate made the call. "Audrey? Kate Finder here. Good news. We have her current location. Gina Lamartina is in Mountain View Hospital, south of Nashville. Hospitals aren't allowed to disclose the reason patients have been admitted. Given her condition and the timing, my best guess is she is delivering or about to. At any rate, you have what you asked for."

Syd and Audrey booked a flight. Their plan was to fly BWI into Nashville and catch a short flight to McGee-Purdue regional airport. It was close to Mountain View Hospital. From there they'd rent a minivan and go directly to the hospital.

Audrey approached reception and asked for the room phone number for Gina Lamartina. She'd taken a selfie of her and Syd standing in front of the *Mountain View* sign at the entrance to the hospital. She texted it to Gina's cell, in hopes Gina unblocked them.

"Hello?" Gina was in between contractions. Her attending physician was pleased the process had started. He told Gina everything was going to be just fine.

"Hi ,Gina. Guess who? It's Audrey. Syd and I can't wait to see you and our baby. We're just so thrilled our new little baby girl will be back in Annapolis with us soon."

"Wait, what? Where are you?" Gina was confused. How did they know she was here, in this hospital, close to delivering? How could they have found her?

"We're right here, darling, at Mountain View, downstairs. We won't be leaving without *our* baby. You just relax and in a few days this will all be over."

"You can't be serious, Audrey. Take my baby? Have you lost your fucking mind? Go back home. You two aren't welcome here. And don't think for a minute you're going to see my baby. Over my dead body, bitch."

"Now, now, calm down. You'll be well taken care of. We'll get you a car and set up a five twenty-nine fund for the children. You can come to the Country Club with us."

"Fuck you, the fund, car, and the Country Club. You're not listening!"

"Well. There's no need to get vulgar. Hear this: we'll get a court ordered paternity test completed. Guess what? Syd is the baby's father. Remember? Oh, maybe you forgot? Let this be your reminder. Whether you like it or not, we have legal rights and we will exercise those rights."

Gina was at a loss for words. She held the receiver limply and hung up.

Jamey and Lily slept for what he thought had been just a few hours in the waiting room. He realized it'd been more than a few hours. He'd given Gina his cell in case she needed anything. The buzz in his pocket startled him. "Gina?" He'd entered her room number in his contacts.

"Jamey. There's a white middle aged couple in the lobby. It's them. They just called me. They…they found me…and they want my baby."

54

Frequently Bad Information

Danielle Rogers was a veteran. Her work with the behavioral unit at Quantico took her all over the country. Working for the FBI's profiling unit was her life. When the fourth woman was found in the Smoky Mountain woods, having been sexually assaulted, strangled to death and branded, her office was asked to assist in the investigation. Danielle would've preferred to be in charge after the second homicide. Unfortunately, local law enforcement rarely asked for help that early in a serial killer case.

Bob was once again called into Corporal Creed's office. He assumed the position in the God awful torturous chair that faced the Corporal's desk.

"She wants a copy of your file. The Erik Stryker file."

Danielle Rogers had arrived early. She commandeered office space and set up shop. Her requisition for supplies and administrative assistance were covered. The homicide unit was scheduled to meet with her to bring her up to date. She noticed a television station van parked at the far end of the parking lot as she surveyed her new outpost from the single window in the office.

Bob was curious. "Why does she want the Stryker file. Thought she was here for the dead girls, you know, the ones with the roses in their mouths? What's Erik Stryker got to do with that?"

"We're the ones who asked for help on this, Bob. You see that reporter in the van out front on your way in? The victim's parents, relatives, the media, the mayor—they're all over this. It's not good. We have to get closure on this one quick. I'm not having a bunch of do-gooders picketing outside. She wants *all* our homicide files, not just yours. She also wants the case files covering geographic areas up to and including Nashville. Nashville alone is twenty detectives and over a hundred fifty homicides last year, Bob. Everything is under scrutiny. I don't pretend to know exactly what she is doing. I just want her to help us catch this maniac and catch a plane back to Quantico. So let's cooperate fully. OK, Bob?"

"OK, Corporal. I'll get it together for her right away. Hope she can read my handwriting."

"Thanks, Bob. I'll be talking to homicide next. I want to make sure they clean up their caseload files before they hand anything over. You know the inside joke the FBI share amongst themselves…. They **F**requently get **B**ad **I**nformation from state and local law enforcement."

"Just to make sure, Corporal, you want me and Bobby to continue running with this one, right?" Corporal Creed knew Bob and Bobby didn't have the correct credentials to investigate a homicide but it was too far along.

"Carry on with your work, Bob. Share every detail no matter how small with Danielle Rogers."

Bob went to his desk and pulled the Erik Stryker file. The Corporal covering his ass again, he thought. He looked over the file and handed it to the department secretary for copying.

The state police department in Sevno County employed two homicide detectives. The four deceased young women, all found in that area, fell under their purview. Due to the nature and importance of these events, the two female detectives were working together. Shannon Dorsey and Michelle Wright went to high school and college together. They received their bachelor degrees in criminal justice within months of each other. After graduating, the two young women joined the police force in Nashville. They completed the required training and gained valuable experience with casework they'd been assigned to. Within two years they were promoted to detective of homicide. When several retirements created openings in Sevno County, they were able to secure transfers. The first year on the job there they each settled forty percent of their assignments. They were disappointed in that statistic. They were also appalled that seventy percent of their convictions were African American men. They knew they couldn't change the stats; they could only work harder and be as fair as the law would allow.

The detectives saw the pattern emerging early on. They were certain they were dealing with the same killer in each case. None of the crime scene details had been leaked to the press. A copycat killer wasn't being considered in the second, third, and fourth murder. They were diligent. Working with forensics at the crime scenes, Michelle's task was to help find and secure physical evidence. Forensics collected fingerprints, bodily fluids, hair samples and took detailed pictures of the crime scenes. Michelle assisted and searched the surrounding area looking for additional evidence. Shannon focused on interviews. She researched each victim's background thoroughly. The parents, siblings, cousins, bosses, coworkers and love interests were all meticulously questioned. She was looking for anything that might link the women together aside from their strikingly similar appearance. Shannon was frustrated. Aside from two of the victims having been in the same grade in the same high school, there were no connections among them.

Danielle Rogers welcomed Michelle and Shannon into her temporary office. She was very pleased she'd be working with a female team. Danielle knew that women tended to be superior to men when it came to the meticulous, methodical approach that cases such as this demanded. She'd spent the prior evening reviewing each case file.

"Good morning, detectives. Welcome to the dark side." Danielle consistently used this greeting when meeting homicide detectives for the first time. "I've read your biographies. It's a pleasure meeting you two. We will make an awesome team. I also spent last night and this morning going over each victim's case file. I'm impressed with your work. I don't often see cases that have been investigated this thoroughly. Before I start, do you have any questions?" They shook their heads in unison. "OK, let us begin."

"I read that you and Michelle ran a sex offender registry list for a thirty-mile radius of the crime scene and that you located and interviewed individuals that were convicted of sexually violent crimes. That was outstanding and is a solid start. Since that didn't turn up anything, I'd like you to expand the area out an additional five miles. Granted, that is a stretch. Most stay close to home. The 'who are we looking' for is near standard textbook, in my opinion. Late twenties to early thirties. Lower middle class background. A sad history of physical, sexual, and more importantly, emotional abuse. A parent, parents or guardian's drug or alcohol dependency could be a contributing factor. Lacks empathy, displays superficial charm, and has no remorse. As the victims were sexually assaulted we can safely assume he enjoys the dominance and power the assault provides him with. He 'feels' something as he is assaulting these women. I said 'he' not because *all* serial killers are male. Obviously this one is. You'll notice I didn't say 'white.' That is a stereotype of serial killers that simply isn't true. I'm guessing that there isn't anything I've said that you didn't already know. So, now you tell me what you know."

"Thanks, Danielle." Michelle opened her notebook and began." Never hurts to educate. We're sure you saw the file pictures. As you know, each woman was raped. Semen was found internally and externally on the bodies. The gags used were identical on number one through three and a different material was used on number four. The circle symbols burned into each victim's breasts were made by the same piece of steel. The outer edge of the marks has a consistent variation. The way the numbers are aligned inside the circles is consistent with the use of several different tools. They vary in size and thickness. The bodies were posed with a rose placed in the mouth. The colors of the roses were primary colors for one through three—red, blue and green. Woman number four had a white rose between her teeth. As you know, they were all strangled to death. The medical examiner report shows the ligature marks are nearly identical. There were no clothes at the crime scenes. There were drag marks and tire tracks found near every scene. Molds were made. The tire tracks are all terrain and all the same. The tread is consistent with a Goodyear product used on late model Jeeps, from what we can determine. The consensus is the women were moved. Whoever did this wasn't careful about where he put these women. Hikers, hunters, birdwatchers—just about anyone could and did, stumble across them."

"Thanks, Michelle. Looks like our killer put out the trash instead of covering up his crimes."

55

No Soliciting

Candy knew there wasn't time to call Scorp. The man outside wasn't just going to leave without some answers. He rang the doorbell again. "OK…alright…I'm gonna open the door. Don't shoot." Candy unlocked the door and opened it slowly. She put her hands up.

"Where the fuck is Scorp? I know he lives here. I want my money now. Tell him to come out!"

"Hold on…hold on…look…he's not here. Come in and we can talk about the money. I know all about it. I'm Candy. You must be Abe. Just come in. Relax."

Abe kept the Browning leveled at Candy's head. The machine pistol was in his other hand. He walked into the foyer and looked around. "Yeah, that's right. I'm Abe. How do I know he ain't hiding somewhere?"

"You don't." Candy grabbed the barrel of the shotgun, pushed it down and away, pivoted and caught him square in the face with her right foot. He fell back, dropping both guns. Blood from his shattered nose and crumbled teeth streamed down his face, chin, and neck. Abe bounced off the doorway. Candy stepped right and landed a liver kick. He tumbled down the steep front steps and landed head first on the sidewalk, splitting the back of his head. "You fuckin' piece of shit! Who the fuck you think you are comin' here." Blood was pooling around his head. Candy realized she'd been screaming at an unconscious man.

Candy could feel the adrenaline pumping. She fished Abe's key fob out of his pocket and ran to his SUV. Working fast she opened the doors and hatch. It took less than five minutes to find and unload the weapons in the back of Abe's Expedition, open the garage, and transfer everything into her minivan. Abe hadn't stirred. She left the shotgun and machine pistol lying inside the front door. She knelt down and checked for a pulse. He was breathing and his pulse felt normal. She ran inside and put a folded kitchen towel under his head, propping it up a few inches. His left arm was lodged at a strange angle halfway behind his back. She lifted his shoulder and gently repositioned his arm.

"911. What's your emergency?"

"There's a man hurt at my house." She gave the dispatcher the address. "I need an ambulance, right now. He's knocked out on the ground and bleeding. Please hurry! And I need the police. The guy that's hurt tried to get into my house. He has guns. Please hurry!"

The dispatcher used the best version of his soothing voice. "OK…OK…they're on the way, Miss. What's your name? Stay on the phone with me. Are you hurt? They are eight minutes away."

"It's Candy. I'm not hurt. Have to go…."

Khloe handed her ringing phone to Scorp. "Here you go. It's not for me. I guarantee you that." They were getting bored and impatient sitting in their little room at the Streamside Inn.

"Hello…Candy?"

"Yeah. I need you to come to the house. Now .You aren't far away, right?"

"No, maybe fifteen minutes. What's up? You sound all amped up?"

"Abe's here. He's hurt. There's an ambulance and cops coming."

"Abe? How do you know it's Abe?"

"I sorta asked him."

"What happened?"

"He got aggressive and lost."

"I'm coming. You wanna come with me, Khloe?"

"Uh…yeah… Let's go! I can't sit here any longer."

The Type D advanced life support ambulance drove over the mangled gate and backed up to Abe's motionless body. Candy was sitting on the top step, holding an unlit Newport. She'd checked Abe's pulse four or five times while she waited. It was just concern. She knew she wouldn't be able to actually do anything if he stopped breathing. She didn't know CPR.

The paramedics checked Abe's vitals and carefully turned him on his side. They were afraid he might choke. While one held him steady, the other team member opened Abe's mouth. He put a finger in to clear his airway. Using his middle finger, he scooped out a mix of broken teeth and coagulated blood. Satisfied with his work, he turned his attention to the back of Abe's head. He moved the folded kitchen towel aside. Abe's skull looked like it was fractured. The two paramedics hoisted him slowly onto the stretcher and moved him inside the ambulance. They hooked him up to the monitoring instrumentation and called it in.

"Ma'am, what is his age?

Candy shrugged. "Don't know his age. Sorry."

"How long has been unresponsive?"

"I called pretty quick once I saw he was knocked out. No more than fifteen minutes."

"You put that towel under his head?"

"Yeah."

"Well, you probably saved his life. The blood from his broken nose and teeth might have closed off his airway if it hadn't been for you. Some ran out the side of his mouth."

"That's good. Will he be alright?"

"Head injuries are tricky ma'am. I honestly don't know. We're taking him to Mount View. If you want to check on him, he'll be in the emergency room in a half hour, forty-five minutes. He has a wallet, so they'll have his information. We'd better get moving."

"Thanks for getting here so fast."

Bob drove his Explorer across the fence, which was now completely pressed into the asphalt. It'd been a long day and he was nearing home when he'd got the call. Attempted armed robbery. The suspect was injured. He waved the ambulance down as they were leaving. "Mount View?"

"Yes sir. Head injury, broken nose, teeth are knocked out. He's unconscious."

A beat up Honda Accord swooped past him. A man, his face and arms heavily bandaged, and a young woman leapt out and approached the other woman sitting on the top step. Their conversation appeared to be animated. Bob was optimistic he could write up a quick report and get home in time to catch Blue Bloods.

Bob parked next to the Accord. "Evening all. Who made the 911 call?"

"That was me, officer." Candy stood up.

"OK, ma'am, why don't you step down here and walk me through it."

"Well, you see that shotgun and pistol right there inside the door? I was inside. I heard a gunshot. The front widows shook. Then the doorbell rang twice. I looked out the window and saw a man…just his head. I opened the door to see what was going on. Those two guns there were pointed at me. He came at me. I pushed my way in between the guns and pushed him. He fell and hit his head. He was knocked out. I ran and got a towel to put under his head, checked his pulse and called 911."

"I see. So, you've never seen this man before?"

"No sir. Never."

"Right. They took him to Mountain View. I'll be interviewing him when he can talk. I'll take those guns." Bob walked up the steps and into the foyer. He picked up the shotgun and pistol. "Yeah, this shotgun was fired recently. This Glock 19 ain't for hunting animals. He looked around. Rich person's house, he mumbled. The three people standing outside didn't fit this house. The woman's distinctive New Jersey accent didn't fit either.

He put the guns in the Explorer. "OK, I need to see some ID. I'll create the report on my laptop and be on my way. I'll let you know what we find out. I assume you will be pressing charges?"

"I'll let you know." Candy went in, found her purse, and handed Bob her license.

"He's going to be charged whether you want to or not, ma'am. I'll need your formal statement. You'll need to come over to the station tomorrow. I'll be there all afternoon."

Bob turned and looked at the bandaged man and the other woman. "Who are you two?"

Scorp answered. "This is our house." He pointed at Candy. He gestured toward Khloe. "This here's my gir…our friend. Candy called us."

Bob got in the Explorer, adjusted his computer screen, and scratched his head. A guy walks up to a house holding two weapons, fires off a shot, then rings the doorbell? A tiny woman decides to open the door? She "pushes" through guns pointed at her and knocks the guy down the steps? Then she calls 911 and her house partner shows up with another woman? He held up the license. Candise Doubleday.

Candy, Scorp, and Khloe had gone inside. Bob found them in the kitchen. Candy was pulling her sweatshirt off, revealing a pink sports bra and a pierced belly button. Bob's eyes focused momentarily. Her bra was supersized. He placed her license on the island, tipped his hat and headed for the door.

Bob backed the Explorer up to leave. He saw a shotgun shell casing on the ground as he swung around. He got out and retrieved it. OK, anything else? he thought. His headlights lit up the garage as he circled around and tried to leave, again. The massive center garage door was open. As he continued to turn, a purple Challenger with shiny black wheels and a beige or tan minivan were illuminated.

56

Nosy Neighbor

Jo was awake. The midazolam in her system was dwindling. She was wet. Her bladder had emptied. In a few minutes her eyes adjusted to the dim basement light. She realized her hands and feet were bound and her top was missing. A gag had cut into the sides of her mouth. She turned her head. There was a mattress next to the one she was on. A naked woman was lying on her back, perfectly still. She was also bound and gagged. Jo saw something on her breasts. Jo struggled and rolled off the mattress and landed on the filthy linoleum floor. She could see a washer and dryer at the other end of the basement, up against the wall. Jo rolled, stopping to squiggle straight several times and stopped, ending up on her back near the dryer. It was vented outside through a thin piece of cardboard. The cardboard had been duct taped and covered part of the ground level basement window.

She was desperate. She couldn't remember everything that happened. It didn't matter. She had to get free. She drew her knees up against her chest and kicked with all the force she could muster. The flimsy metal dryer let out a loud boom in response. Jo kicked it again and again. The dryer skirted up against the wall, affording her a solid target.

Erik and Quinn's neighbor, who rented the other side of the duplex, wasn't well liked. She spent her days and nights either sitting by the front or rear windows of her house, watching her neighbors up and down the block come and go. She frequently filed complaints with the zoning department, animal welfare, social services, and law enforcement when she saw or heard anything that looked suspicious. Her vivid imagination caused unwarranted attention most times. She was retrieving her trashcans from the alley that ran behind her house when she heard it. She followed the hollow metallic boom. It was coming from the twin's basement. After running around to the front and banging on their front door, she noticed the Jeep was gone. Since they shared the Jeep, one of them could still be home. No one answered. She ran back around the house and pulled her picnic table over to the short chain link fence separating the properties and jumped off into her neighbor's yard. The noise grew louder the closer she drew. The ground level window shook with each rumble. She feared whatever was making that noise might affect her side of the duplex. She kneeled down and used her sleeve to clear off the dirt obscuring her view. She could see the top of an appliance and a blonde woman's head.

"911. What's your emergency?" It was *her*, again. Dispatch was required to be calm, courteous and above all, helpful. That wasn't always easy. She asked for the address. The complaint was unique. The frequent female caller reported a loud noise coming from her neighbor's basement. She could see a woman's head on the basement floor. It had some tape or rope around it.

"Can you see if the woman is breathing? Is she in distress?" The dispatcher wasn't sending her guys on some nosy neighbor misunderstanding. Likely a woman grunting away on her Peloton and a reflection distorting the picture. "Is the head attached to a body?" Sometimes you had to be specific, she thought.

"I'm outside their house. I can't see much. You need to send somebody. Something weird going on."

Bob was tired. He hadn't slept well. He was sitting at Double Donuts enjoying his free daily coffee and honey dip. The armed robbery call he'd taken was vexing him. He opened his notebook and turned to his latest entry: Jo Erik Candy Purple Challenger Beige Minivan. Jo appeared to be missing. Erik was dead. Candise was surely the long version of Candy. He'd met a Candise who had a purple Challenger and a beige minivan in her garage. She was wearing an extra large sports bra and had a Jersey accent. His thinking was interrupted. Dispatch called out the complaint and the address. Bob shut his notebook, finished his donut and was on the way. He knew where he was headed. The address was Quinn Stryker's house.

The nosy neighbor met Bob at the curb. When dispatch had announced the 911 caller identity, Bob remembered. She was the quack that was ridiculed by dispatch. Daisy Turnbuckle. He'd been fortunate. He'd never met her. Bobby, on the other hand, had told stories about the times he had to deal with her. Bob took a deep breath.

"Mornin', Ms. Turnbuckle. What seems to be the problem?"

"I just don't know officer. It's my neighbor's house. The Stryker twins house other side of mine."

"Did you say Stryker *twins*?"

"Sure did. They're identical. Spitin' image of each other. Can't tell them apart, and I've been trying."

"I bet you have. So, tell me what's going on, Ms. Turnbuckle."

Bob listened to her story and knocked on the front door for grins. Erik was dead and Quinn was emptying trashcans.

"Told ya." Daisy grinned. "I'll show you around back." She led Bob to the rear of the property and they hopped the fence. "Right in that window there…wait…hear that?"

Bob heard the sound that Daisy called about. He asked her to stand back, twice. He kneeled down and tilted his head to get a better angle. He could just make out the neck and head of a young blonde woman through the filthy window. She appeared to be gagged. He jerked back as the next boom filled his ears. Bob popped up.

"Ms. Turnbuckle, I need you to come with me."

Daisy followed him to his Explorer. "See. I told ya'. There's something strange goin' on in there!"

Bob didn't reply. "Get in." He opened the back door. "Give me your phone. You sit right there. Don't say a word. Do not exit the vehicle. You understand?"

"You don't have to be so mean about it. I'll be quiet." She handed Bob her phone and reluctantly climbed in.

Bob had to think. The gagged woman was in obvious distress He decided. This was way over his pay grade. His days as a fill-in homicide investigator were over. He called for backup and an ambulance. He turned on the Explorer's flashing beacons, reminded Daisy to follow his instructions, stepped out, and called Danielle Rogers.

Danielle Rogers was at a meeting when Bob called. She had put together a war board in her office. Pictures of the murder victims were displayed across the top. Michelle Wright and Shannon Dorsey were assembling a timeline. They'd already done this once, but Danielle wanted them to review it again and then add it to the board.

"Ms. Rogers? I'm sorry to interrupt. Corporal Creed told me to keep you informed about anything I turned up in the Erik Stryker case. So, I'm at the house where Erik lived right now. You may know that his brother Quinn lives here also. I just responded to a neighbor complaint at the Stryker residence.

Danielle cut him off. "Can't this wait? I'm in the middle of an important meeting. I don't need you calling me with this sort of thing—just update the file." She slammed the phone down. "Now where were we?" Michelle and Shannon looked at each other in disbelief. Michelle mouthed "What a bitch."

57

Nothing Has Worked Out

Candy didn't feel safe. The Abe incident only solved half of their problem. They didn't know where Jamey was.

"You think Jamey's up next with more weapons, Scorp? Scorp and Candy were trying to piece it all together. They were still in the kitchen. The state policeman had finished and left hours ago.

"Let me think, Candy. I could use a drink." Khloe wanted to interrupt. Drinking and Oxy didn't mix well. She thought better of it.

"Me too, Scorp. Candy broke out a bottle of Grey Goose. She got three glasses out and added vodka to ice.

"I'd say cheers but it don't match our situation." Khloe was perplexed. Candy just made her a drink and smiled at her. She was too shocked to react.

Candy had her elbow on the island and was holding her glass close to her mouth as she made love to her drink. "Khloe, I wanna say I'm sorry for how I've been treating you. I want you to know I'm grateful for everything you've done for Scorp. I was thinking about it—you made a simple deal to bring Scorp here and your world's been blown up because of it. It isn't fair to you."

Khloe wasn't sure where Candy was going with her speech. On one hand she sounded genuine. On the other she may be encouraging her to get in her car and leave. Not that that hadn't crossed her mind more than once.

"Um, thanks, Candy. I still have a condo and a good job waiting for me back home. And my mom's there. I did think I'd be on my way back by now. I'm a nurse so taking care of Scorp comes natural to me. It's what I do. And until tonight I haven't been scared or worried. I think seeing those guns freaked me out."

"Since you're a nurse and all, maybe you could answer some questions for me later?" Candy had her legs crossed and was swinging one leg. She noticed the top her sock was coated with dried blood. Khloe noticed also.

"What happened to your foot! Let me take a look at it." Khloe got off her stool and kneeled down to get a better look. "This what you have questions about?"

"Oh, no…no. Not that. My foot's OK." Candy tapped Khloe's shoulder. "Really, it's OK, but thanks." She crossed her legs in the opposite direction.

Scorp just sipped his drink and watched them banter. He knew what caused Candy's right sock to be encrusted with blood. It was on *top* of her sock. She hadn't walked through blood to get that on her sock. He didn't see Abe before they loaded him in the ambulance. Scorp was sure Abe's face had been hit hard with a size five. He hadn't been pushed. She'd disarmed him and kicked him, hard. Probably several times.

"So, Scorp, I got off track. What about Jamey? If Abe knows where we live, Jamey knows too. Not sure why he didn't show up here with Abe. I mean, Jamey gets half the money, so why wouldn't he have come tonight too?"

Scorp finished off his vodka. He looked at Candy. "Simple. It's Gina. I've been around Jamey enough. If he's been around her for a couple days he's interested, even if she's pregnant. He ain't a bad person. He's no Abe."

"I don't know why I didn't think of that. So, what's next?"

"Me and Khloe go back to the Streamside and get some sleep. You have a date with that grumpy cop."

"Stay here tonight, Scorp. There are enough bedrooms for the three of us."

Khloe wasn't turning that offer down. A real bed and a real bathroom.

She was almost asleep when she heard a soft knock at her bedroom door. "Scorp? You OK?" Khloe raised her head off the pillow.

"It's me, Khloe. Can I ask you a few questions now?"

Khloe got up and opened the bedroom door. "Sure. No problem at all. Sit with me, Candy."

"I…I, well, you know I was attacked. I went to get tested. I had a voicemail from my doctor today. She said I have HIV and Hepatitis C. I'm scared. I was talking to my friend Jo about this kind of stuff, but I can't reach her. I don't know what I should do. Thought maybe since you're a nurse…."

"You can go to an ER. Hospitals carry the meds you need. They definitely can get you started right away on the HEP C medication. I know there is a med called PEP that's good for HIV. I think you should start taking it within seventy-two hours of infection. Has it been longer than that?"

"I don't know. Ever since I got here…it's all running together. Nothing's worked out."

"I'm sorry, Candy. I'll go with you if you want."

"OK." Candy threw her arms around her and pulled her close. When she let go, Khloe saw a single tear.

58

I Need Your Help

Bob was still in shock. The short conversation he'd had with Danielle Rogers left him reeling. Backup and an ambulance were going to be arriving in minutes. There was a gagged and bound young woman who needed immediate attention in the basement. He'd just found out Erik and Quinn were identical twins. If he went in the house and fucked up the crime scene, he'd be fired. If he didn't get in that house quickly, the young woman might die. He had to act fast.

Corporal Creed picked up. "Corporal, it's Bob. I'm at the Stryker house. There's a woman on Stryker's basement floor who's been gagged. I have an ambulance and backup on the way. I called that asshole Danielle Rogers…she hung up on me. Can you get Michelle Wright and Shannon Dorsey over here STAT. And a forensics team. Dispatch has the address. I'm going in."

"Sure thing Bob. I'm on it."

"That's telling 'em!" He'd forgotten about his passenger.

"You didn't hear any of that. You hear me! I'll have you arrested for obstruction of justice if you repeat any of that to anybody. I'll make sure you do twenty years!"

Bob snatched his Hooligan bar from the back of the Explorer, ran around to the rear of the house, jumped the fence, and went to work. The basement door was old and weak. He had it open in seconds. He hurried over to her. Jo had passed out from the exertion. Bob pulled his pocket knife out and carefully cut the gag from behind her head. Seconds later her eyes opened.

"Who did this to you? What's your name?"

"Name's Jo. I don't know for sure. He was young, white. Looked like the doorman at Club 654…."

"Help's on the way. Hang on for me…hang on." He cut her hands free. Jo pointed behind him. Her arm dropped from weakness. "There…there…." She raised her arm again. Bob sucked in hard when he saw another woman on a mattress across the room. He approached the woman. She was naked, bound, and gagged. Her eyes were open… lifeless. There were ligature marks on her throat. She had circles and numbers branded on her breasts. Her legs were spread. He spotted some metal rods and a propane torch on the floor. One of the rods had a circle attached to it.

Backup consisting of one officer parked behind Bob's Explorer. As the officer walked up to the house, a muffled voice from Bob's truck startled him, proclaiming, "He's out back! Go around!"

"Holy Mother of God!" Bob heard his backup before he saw him. Two paramedics entered the basement next. Bob told them that Jo was alive, but in and out of consciousness. He pointed to the dead woman. "She's dead. Homicide is on the way." Bob clambered up the basement stairs…and threw up.

Michelle Wright and Shannon Dorsey drove to the Stryker house together. Danielle Rogers was furious that they followed Corporal Creed's directive. They met with Bob at his truck to consult. Michelle spotted Daisy Turnbuckle with her ear pressed up against the window of Bob's Explorer.

"Who the fuck is that, Bob?" Michele motioned to the gray head in the back of Bob's truck.

"Oh. Sorry. She is the 911'er. I'll get rid of her." He opened the door, gave her phone back and pointed to her house. "Go in. Stay away from windows and don't make any calls. Understood?"

"OK. Harsh thing, aren't you?"

Bob turned back to the detectives. "We'll need to get together formal-like I guess but I'll try to fill you in quick. First off, the only reason I'm involved is because Corporal Creed asked me to follow Erik Stryker's case to completion. His thinking was it would free you two so you could focus on the serial killer. You have the

Stryker file. I was at this house once before to notify next of kin about Erik's death. Quinn Stryker identified his dead brother at the morgue. I didn't know Erik and Quinn were twins much less identical twins until their neighbor told me… today. I didn't have no reason to believe either of them had anything to do with those poor women. I was just trying to find who killed Erik. I got the 911 call for this." Bob made a wide arc with his arm. The neighbor led me to the back and I saw one of the women through a window. She was on the basement floor kickin' the clothes dryer. That's why the neighbor called to begin with—the noise. Anyways, I broke the door down and checked on the girl. She's awake off and on. I cut off her gag and ties. That's all I did. I didn't touch her body or move her around. Her name is Jo. She said the man that did this to her looked like Erik Stryker. She said he worked at Club 654, which is right, he did work there. The other woman down there is dead. Looks like she was strangled, maybe raped, and branded. I didn't touch…move, anything."

Michelle had been nodding in agreement while Bob talked. "Nice job, Bob. It started as a routine call. You made the best of it. We need to find Quinn. Bring him in. Question the girl who survived. Shannon and I will work with forensics… process the entire scene top to bottom. It's critical we get it right. Do you have any idea where Quinn might be? Know what he drives?" Shannon waved to the forensic group as their van lined up behind them.

"He works at Double Donuts. Saw him there the other day. Drives a white four-door Jeep with giant tires on it."

"We'll put out a BOL on him right now, Bob. Why don't you take a break? Me and Shannon got this. We'll find him."

"Thanks, Michelle. Appreciate it. I'm going in to the office. I have a meeting with a home invasion victim this afternoon and then I'm heading home."

59

White Collared

Jim Griot wanted his lawyer, Janice Barnes, to be in court representing him for his arraignment hearing. He'd been arrested at Essential Sales & Rental under a warrant for felony corporate fraud. The Bank Two inventory audit showed equipment listed as rented on the books was falsified. A CAT front end loader was unaccounted for. Bank Two investigators provided prosecutors with documents that were then shown to the grand jury that was convened. There were two witnesses questioned. Laura Morningstar and Paul Grim testified on behalf of the prosecution. The vote was unanimous and found Jim liable. He was arrested under warrant without incident. His employees were sent home and his business was locked down.

Laura Morningstar was the whistleblower. She searched for and found the inventory discrepancy and called her lover Paul Grim at Bank Two. They met and planned a course of action. If their plan succeeded, Laura would be the new owner of Essential Sales & Rental, and Jim Griot would be behind bars. Paul Grim was hesitant at first. He would need to call for an unscheduled audit. He'd need to discuss that with management. Laura was pressuring him. Their weekly meetups had become strategy sessions mixed with uninhibited sex. He'd divorce his wife and marry the new president of the largest equipment supplier in the state. They'd grow the business and grow old together.

Janice advised Jim to plead guilty. If additional charges appeared, the guilty plea would insulate him. He'd been in a holding cell for forty-eight hours.

"Is there anything we can do to get me out of this, Janice? I just needed a little more time to straighten things out. I was going to fix it. I needed money for my parents' care. I'm not a crook. Do you know why that audit was sprung on me like that?"

"First off, Jim, I know you're not some evil master crook. As far as why the bank surprised you I can't say. The prosecution had at least two grand jury witnesses. Their identities are kept confidential. I can't negotiate with the Assistant States Attorney, Jim. There is no exculpatory evidence to present. You're charged with a felony, so pretrial diversion is not on the table. And filing a motion with the judge to dismiss would be wasting my time and your money.

"It was Laura Morningstar. I should have figured that out. She's fucking Paul Grim, the bank auditor, Janice."

"You haven't seen the news. Her fucking days are over. She's dead."

"What? What happened? They know what happened to her?"

Janice told him what she'd heard regarding the Laura Morningstar murder. "There was another woman found with her, Jim. Jo Brooks. She survived the ordeal."

"That's fantastic news about Jo, Janice. Too bad about Laura though. She didn't deserve that. What kind of a monster would do such a thing? How do we go forward now?"

"We go through the process together. You don't have any priors. White collar crimes are looked upon differently. There aren't any victims harmed physically. It's just money. You will be released soon on bail. I'll post it for you at the preliminary hearing. At the right time, we present our case for restitution and supervised probation. That could mean you lose everything but you'd avoid any jail time. You come up with the full restitution amount and hopefully you just pay an additional fine and keep your business. Finding financing going forward may mean you take on solid partners. So, agree to pay the bank back and pay the fine imposed, which could be a substantial dollar figure. Any way you can come up with that much money?"

"Yeah, there's a way. Just get me out of here."

60

Mount View Mayhem

Khloe couldn't sleep. She kept looking at her phone to see how much sleep she wasn't getting. It was no use trying, she thought. She, Scorp, and Candy went to bed early after finishing their drinks. Khloe tried to comfort and advise Candy later when she came to her bedroom with questions. Khloe's day had been unsettling. She turned on the TV in the bedroom and caught the local news. Two women had been found in the basement of a house. Details of their confinement were not being released to the public. They'd been identified as Jo Brooks and Laura Morningstar. Both local women. Laura Morningstar was pronounced dead at the scene. Jo Brooks had been transported to Mountain View. Her condition wasn't known. The segment concluded with the reporter interviewing special agent Danielle Rogers, FBI.

It was small talk. Khloe, Candy, and Scorp were groggy. None of them slept well. Khloe was showing Candy how to treat and cover Scorp's injuries properly.

"You guys see the news last night?"

"Remember? I hate news. Never anything good. Depresses me." Scorp turned to Khloe. "Why, what's going on? Something we should know about?"

"No, they just dropped a story about two local women found tied up in some basement around here somewhere. One was dead and one was sent to Mountain View. Didn't think stuff like that happened around here. It's so peaceful."

Candy perked up. "Wow, they say who did it or who the women were?"

"I remember the one name. It was Jo Brooks. The dead woman worked at some big rental company. They put up a picture of a suspect. He owned the house they were found in. I think his name is Stryker. It stuck in my head. You know—'strike her.'"

"Erik Stryker, Khloe? Jo Brooks! Oh no. Geez."

"No, his name wasn't Erik. it was Quinton or Quinn. Not sure."

"Maybe it's a relative of Erik."

"Who's Erik Stryker, Candy? Ain't never heard that name. Where you know him from?" Scorp was scowling.

"Never mind, Scorp. It ain't important. But Jo Brooks. Don't you remember, Khloe? You met Jo. Right here."

"Hmm, now that you mention it, yeah. They didn't show any pictures of the women. So much has been happening. I'm having a rough time processing. Makes nursing look easy."

"So, they said Jo was taken to Mountain View?"

"Yeah. They didn't give any more information. You know, one of those developing story deals."

"Scorp, we need to get to Mountain View. Candy looked at Khloe. That trip had already been discussed last night, for different reasons. Scorp didn't need to know about that just yet. Candy was upset. Her new bff was hurt and in the hospital. Could have been killed. She had to see her. Make sure she was going to be OK.

They took Khloe's car. The ride to Mountain View was quick and quiet. Khloe drove with Scorp riding shotgun. Candy was smoking a Newport and watching the trees fly by. She wasn't sure how she felt about anything. Scorp was certainly taken with Khloe. He couldn't hide it. And Khloe was just one of those rare people that you just had to like. Candy was thinking about the chaos that surrounded her for as far back as she could remember. The move to Tennessee did nothing to improve her life. Chaos had followed her and was slowly destroying her. Her move south with Scorp was supposed to simplify their way of living. It had the opposite effect. Her phone chimed and changed her focus.

"Hello? Jim? Is that you?"

"Yeah. Hi. I saw you called."

"I'm putting you on speaker, Jim. Scorp is with me. Where have you been! I was worried about you. What happened? Why did you flake on us?"

"I'm sorry, Candy. Long story. Got arrested but I'm out now. I'm ready to do the job. When can I start?" Jim had the equipment and a utility body truck at the ready. He'd been ready to go the day he was cuffed.

"Today if you can, Jim. We'll be back later and I'll call you. The gate around the house is busted. You can go over now if you want and wait."

"I'll do that. See you guys soon." Jim loaded up the burner bar and all the equipment he'd need for the task.

Jamey and Lily left the Streamside Inn. Their Uber driver was happy to see her new repeat customers again. She took the side entrance to the hospital, passing the emergency room entrance. Two paramedics were unloading a stretcher. Jamey glanced over and looked again. It was Abe. He recognized the beard and the spider web tattoo on his neck. Judging from the damage to his face, his strong arm tactics with Scorp had failed. They entered the hospital and saw a long line of visitors waiting to be badged. He wouldn't be able to check on Gina. She wasn't answering her room phone. He guided Lily over to a visitor seating area near the main lobby entrance.

Syd and Audrey were back, sitting on a bench near the elevators in the hospital lobby. Syd told Audrey he didn't want to stay another night at the Streamside Inn. He wanted to find a better motel. Audrey wasn't listening. Audrey was insisting that they try to see Gina. She thought standing in front of her might help change Gina's mind. Come back to Annapolis when their daughter was born. Syd didn't think that would help. Might even hurt their chances of a civil conclusion. He'd already had one spirited argument today with Audrey over their accommodations. Another "discussion" with his feisty wife wasn't on his agenda.

Sam and Dave, the brothers who attacked Candy, were not doing well. Their dehydration improved and the dentist on call had pulled their remaining teeth. The ankle and arm restraints were removed. Neither brother was lucid. Antipsychotics were keeping them still, slowing the onslaught of hallucinations. The hospital social worker reached out and contacted their mother. Tracy Lynne drove the old lady to see her sons and decide their future. Her sons fell within the twenty percent of longtime methamphetamine abusers that would never be well enough to rejoin society. Tracy Lynne parked her truck on the visitor lot across the street from Mountain View. She opened her big purse, handed a pipe and a baggie of meth shards to her passenger, and a cloud of smoke filled the cab. She waited for the bowl to cool and filled it again, this time for her. "Ah…momma, let's go." They entered the lobby and found one of the benches lining the glass walled reception area. Their appointment was twenty minutes away.

Candy, Khloe, and Scorp entered the main entrance to the hospital. A young woman using a walker was at the reception desk. There was a line of a dozen or more backed up behind the woman, waiting. Some of them were trying to control their small children. The feeble young woman was raising her voice and shaking her finger at the receptionist. A security guard made his way over and stood off to the side. This was going to take some time. Candy frowned. "Let's sit this one out, Scorp." They chose a sofa with a clear view of the reception line.

Khloe hadn't eaten all day. She wondered how Scorp survived sometimes. He hardly ate anything. A bagel or a burger now and then. She was starved. "Hey, let's get some snacks. There's some vending machines over there. We can snack here. We can see what's going on if we stay here. We don't have to go to the cafeteria."

"I'll fly an' buy." Candy scrabbled around in her coat pockets. "Got some ones and a ton a change. Cheez-Its, Cheetos, Doritos, and some sodas coming up." She was still focusing on organizing her money as she walked toward the vending area. Her peripheral vision alerted her to a problem.

"It's her, look, it's that bitch Candy."

Candy caught fast movement in her peripheral vison. Tracy Lynne and her friend leapt up and darted toward Candy. They were super high. Their energy level was in the stratosphere. Tracy Lynne tackled her. The old woman was screaming and flailing away randomly. Candy fell backwards and hit her head on the polished marble floor. Scorp stood up when he saw the ruckus. Khloe stood too and reached for his hand. "No, you can't."

The lone security guard looked like a statue that had seen a ghost. Before he moved, Candy reacted. She raised her knees slightly and drove her elbow into Tracy Lynne's head. Seeing no immediate reaction, Candy rolled and wrapped her arm around Tracy Lynne's neck. She gripped her wrists together, jerked her arm tight, and held on. By the time the security guard reached them, Tracy Lynne was lying face down and motionless. Turning her attention to the pest trying to hit her, Candy stood up, grabbed her arms and swung her around, releasing her in the direction of the security officer. The security guard caught her and wrapped his arms around her in a bear hug. She was still trying to fight with somebody. Candy knelt down. She'd timed her hold on Tracy Lynne. Long enough to incapacitate her but not long enough to kill her. She turned her over gently, lifted her head and pressed down on her chest, moving her body from side to side. Tracy Lynne opened her eyes. She was disoriented. Candy helped her up and walked her over to the bench she'd been sitting on. She helped her sit and whispered in her ear. "Stay put. Don't move. You'll be just fine in a minute. Don't try that again, babe."

Jamey saw the commotion. He wasn't sure how it would end. He'd seen too many simple fistfights turn into gunfire. He wasn't taking any chances. He couldn't get past the fight going on in the lobby with Lily. He looked around for a place to hide her. Then, the idea hit him. "Ma'am, excuse me. Could you take my daughter into the ladies' room for me until this mess is over? Please? I don't know what else to do."

"Why, of course young man. I'd be happy to help you." Audrey took Lily by the hand and led her away. She put a finger to her lip. "Shh…let's play a game. Just you and me, like we used to." Lily smiled. Audrey was a familiar friendly face. Once inside, Audrey called Syd on his cell. He'd heard the lobby fight but couldn't see much from where he was sitting, so he turned his attention back to the latest issue of *Golf Digest*. "Yeah, what now, Audrey?"

"Shh…I have Lily. I'll explain later. Pull the van around to the rear entrance. I'll meet you there. Hurry, Syd."

The huge security guard kept his bear hug grip on the meth brothers' mother. Three more guards walked through the swinging doors at the end of the hall. They'd seen everything on the monitors in the break room. The big guy barked. "You three! Outside! You, Miss! Outside! Now!" He pointed at Candy, Khloe, Scorp, and Tracy Lynne. He carried his captive, and the other guards escorted everyone out. "Now, here's the deal." He put the old lady down next to Tracy Lynne. "You two started it. I saw it all. I should have you arrested for assault and battery. You are leaving. Right now. If I ever see you here again it won't be fun for you. Now git!" He turned to Candy. "That was something else young lady. Thank you for making my job easier. If you'd killed them it would have caused lots of paperwork. If ya'll don't have a critical need to be here, I'm gonna suggest you come back tomorrow during visiting hours."

Jamey was standing at the entrance, watching the spectacle unwind. He couldn't be sure what was happening from where he was standing. The man with the bandaged face looked like Scorp in a way. He walked outside to get closer and he saw the scorpion tattoos. It was him. Jamey put his hands up and closed the twenty-five feet that separated them.

"Scorp! Is that you? It's me, Jamey."

"Yeah. It's me. Back off! What are you doing here? Don't have what I owe you on me, but I have it. This here's Candy. I told you and Abe about her, remember?"

Candy stepped forward and stood in front of Scorp." I just got out of a fight, Jamey. I don't wanna get into another. I'm not sure why you are here, unless it's to see you buddy Abe. I fucked his face up and he's got a room inside. We don't want any trouble. You'll have your money tomorrow." Candy thought she summed it up pretty well. "You know where we live. Stop by tomorrow. Alone. It will all be just fine." She took his phone and entered her cell digits.

"Look ,I'm here because Gina Lamartina's having her baby. We were traveling with Abe. He's deserted us. I saw what happened to his face. We found Gina while searching for you two, in Annapolis. She wanted to come with us. We didn't force her. OK? Look, I don't want any trouble. I ain't Abe. I can come to your place sometime tomorrow. As long as it's safe for Lily. I'm watching her for Gina."

"Where is Lily?"

"A lady has her inside. I had her take Lily into the ladies' room while you were wrestling with those freaks."

"Oh, OK. We're taking off, Jamey. Give our best to Gina. Tell her we'll be back soon to see her. You have my cell. Scorp is cell free these days. We'll see you tomorrow." Candy wanted to see Gina. It was difficult leaving without visiting her.

Scorp believed Jamey. He'd always been truthful. They had nothing to fear from him. It appeared Jamey's priorities had shifted to Gina.

As they walked to her Accord, Khloe stopped and turned. "Who were those crazy women, Candy?" Me and Scorp have been wondering if that was just random shit."

"They're related to the men that raped me. I ran into both of them bitches the day I was attacked. I don't really know why they reacted like that. I never did anything to them." Candy wished she could be honest about it. If the group of freaks were ever charged in Erik Stryker's death, she'd share the details with Scorp and Khloe of how she framed them. They deserved to go to jail. She didn't care how they got there.

61

Stryke Out

Quinn Stryker left work at Double Donuts early. His plan was to head home, wait for darkness, and take dead Laura Morningstar for a nice ride in the country. He'd thought about how good it felt raping and branding her. It felt almost as good as watching her eyes forming blood spots as he strangled the last breath out of her body. The other one could wait. He wouldn't mind a few days alone with her before killing her. He stopped at the florist he frequented and bought four roses—primary colors. He sprayed them with a clear sealant as he'd done in the past. The roses would then last longer than the dead women.

As he drove, he turned on the radio and heard it. There was an alert being broadcasted. They were looking for him. Maybe he'd been careless? His patience had deserted him and his execution was sloppy lately. He always did better when he worked together with his brother Erik. Erik was his rock. He never panicked. He was meticulous. They'd planned on moving soon. Just a few more blondes and then they were moving to Florida. Erik's death was such a shock. Seeing his bloated face in the morgue was unbearable. How did that happen? Why was he behind that store? Erik was texting him after he left the Club early that night. Erik's texts were arousing. He'd met two blondes and was alone with them. He would text when he was ready. He was preparing to kill the first one. Number two was asleep. They'd have a night to remember. The pictures he'd promised never came through. He stopped communicating. What happened to ruin the plans they had made?

Michelle Wright and Shannon Dorsey were following Quinn. A white Jeep was not a hard vehicle to find. When they learned

Quinn had left Double Donuts a few minutes before they got there, they knew it was just a matter of minutes before they had him in custody. A half mile ahead, they saw the Jeep. Michelle floored the unmarked Explorer ST and closed in. Shannon requested back-up. She flipped the light bar on and engaged the siren. The Jeep was slowing down. Michelle was praying this wouldn't be an OJ Simpson show. The Jeep pulled over and stopped. The exhaust vapor told the detectives the engine was running. He could still run. They could see flashing lights behind them. They estimated backup was a minute out. They'd try to wait. Michelle could see Quinn's head in his side view mirror. Shannon reached into the rear seat and brought her Remington eight-seventy shotgun to rest on her lap. The eighteen-inch barreled gun was loaded with double-O buckshot. Michelle was gripping her standard issue Glock. Just as the two Mustang interceptors skidded to a stop behind them, they heard the shot from Quinn's forty-five caliber handgun. The driver's side window blew out in a bright cloud of red.

Corporal Creed asked Danielle Rogers to come to his office. He gave her the news. His homicide department had solved the serial murder case. The suspect, Quinn Stryker, the identical twin of Erik Stryker, shot himself. Danielle asked if she was needed to wrap up the case. She reminded him that twin DNA is identical. "It will take a considerable amount of high level expertise to determine which brother killed these women, Corporal."

"Ms. Rogers, please gather up your posters and pictures and leave. Your services, if you can call them that, are no longer needed." The heat was off Corporal Creed.

62

The Other Door

Candy drove. Scorp and Khloe were sleeping. She cracked her window and lit a Newport. She stubbed it out in the ashtray, dropped the window lower, and tossed it out. She was trying to quit. Tired of being the outcast wherever she went.

Her phone interrupted her thoughts. It was Jamey.

"Lily's gone. I've looked everywhere. That woman must have her. What am I gonna do?"

"You check the cafeteria and the children's playroom and outside? Maybe they went for a walk. Look, Jamey, we'll be back in a couple hours or so. If you don't find her by then we'll call the police and report it, OK?"

"OK…alright, I'll keep looking."

Jamey made a second trip to the security office. He'd asked them to take a look at the footage from the last half hour. "There… there she is. That's the woman. That's Lily! That must be her husband with them. Where are they?"

"They used the other door, sir. The rear entrance. They're on lot four." On the monitor they could see the bright red Toyota Sienna van drive around the circle, across the rear entrance drive, and park.

"How long ago was this?" Jamey could see the license plate. It was out of state. They either drove here or it was a rental.

"Twenty-five minutes ago."

Jamey rushed back to reception. He'd let Gina down. It had to have been that couple that called Gina. How could he have been so careless? And how could he tell Gina? He called Candy.

Jim backed up the Chevy Kodiak to the garage door. He was

glad to see it'd been left open. He could get started. He hooked up the oxygen and oxy-acetylene hoses and carried the bundles of hose down the stairs to vault level. He laid out the hoses carefully. He didn't need to trip over anything once he lit off the burner bar. The pistol grip dead man trigger handle was next. He attached it to the bar and then hauled in two large fans and three fire extinguishers. His protective gear was laid out on the floor. Jim was ready to rumble.

Candy drove up, parked next to Jim's truck, sprang out, and hugged him. She'd driven eighty-five the entire way. "Thank God. I'm so glad you're here. I wanna hear all about your arrest later. We're in a terrible rush. This here is Scorp and Khloe, Jim. We'll move the cars out for you so you can get started."

"Before you move them, I have a question. Walk down there with me."

"Can you unlock it for me? I need to know what's behind it. It's too close to where I'm working." Jim pointed to the Mechanical Room door.

"I'll get the key. It's probably on the key ring in the junk drawer." Candy took the elevator, found the keys, and rushed back down. "Here you go, Jim. It's one of these."

"Here we go." The third key he tried turned the tumbler. He opened the door, felt around and found the light switch. The bright LED lights revealed three hot water heaters, a water softener, and a set of electric service panels. There was a sliding barn style door to his left. Jim pulled the iron handle and walked the door open. The rear wall of the vault was right in front of them. Candy gasped. Jim turned the hand wheel counterclockwise and pushed down on the lever just below it. He exhaled as he braced himself and pulled the heavy door open. He turned and grinned. "Guess somebody forgot to lock the back door." Candy was incredulous. How could they be so dumb? All that time, effort, energy, and angst.... So much of what happened didn't have to happen. For once, she was speechless.

Scorp shook his head. This was all his fault. Everything. None of it could be reversed. He'd be turning this over in his head the rest of his life. He looked over at Candy and saw one single tear.

Candy asked Jim to wait at his truck. While he packed up his equipment, Khloe helped Candy count out one million dollars. They put the money into four plastic tubs. Candy placed two kilos of heroin in a zip up tool bag. They delivered the four tubs to Jim, and Candy threw the tool bag of drugs into Khloe's car. Scorp was intrigued. "What are you doing with that bag of smack, Candy?" His day had introduced him to a splitting headache.

"You'll see."

63

You Know What To Do

"**Let's** go! I'll drive." Candy was speeding back to Mountain View. Khloe was complaining. "If I don't get some food, I'm going to pass out. And I can't do what you want if I'm passed out."

"Good point, girl. There's a Wendy's next exit." Candy had explained to Khloe exactly how to act. It would go smoothly if she stayed calm and didn't raise any suspicions with her actions.

It was Jamey. He was calling Candy in a panic. "I found them. They're in a red Toyota van parked on lot four. I just checked in at reception. Gina had the baby. I think they know that and are waiting, you know, to hold Lily hostage or something. I don't know what to do, Candy. I told security to hold off calling the cops. That it might just be a misunderstanding. That I would take care of it."

"I know what to do, Jamey. Don't approach them, but keep an eye on them. We'll be there soon. I'll call you. Concentrate on Gina. We'll handle Syd and Audrey."

"**There's** the red van, guys. Get going, Scorp." Candy parked next to a large Sprinter van. Audrey and Syd couldn't see the Accord or who was in it. Audrey would recognize Candy. Scorp's bandages disguised him well. He'd put on a dirty nylon jacket to cover his arms. Oily, ripped jeans and untied, worn combat boots completed the look. Candy sprinkled some bottled water on him and mussed his hair.

Scorp put the sign around his neck—*Homeless Vet Hungry Please Help*. He staggered over to the red van. Khloe peeked around the Sprinter and waited. Scorp was gesturing and pleading for a donation. She had to move fast. If Syd moved the van to get away from Scorp, it was game over. Syd was listening to Scorp's speech. Audrey was busy. She was yelling at Syd to roll the window up. She decided to just give the man some cash so he'd go away. She was reaching over the console to get her purse. When she righted herself, the homeless man was limping away and a young woman was standing by her door, waving. "Hi miss. Sorry if I startled you. I'm a nurse here. I noticed you're tire is low on air. I have a little compressor in my car. I can fill it up for you. Just take a few minutes. Just need to plug in to your twelve volt outlet." Khloe was crossing her fingers.

"Well, that's very kind and thoughtful of you, dear. Don't you think so, Syd? That would be great if you could do that for us."

"I'll be right back." Khloe got the mini compressor out of the Accord trunk and picked up the tool bag.

"OK, all set. Just need to hook it up and plug it in. Can you open the hatch? It'll be easier to use the power outlet back here." Syd used the key fob and opened it. Lily was hanging over the second row seat.

"Lily, sit back down. Don't bother this nice lady." Audrey and Syd didn't even get out to inspect the tire. Syd was too busy reading *Sports Illustrated*, and Audrey couldn't tell a tire from a rim.

Khloe plugged the compressor into the twelve-volt hatch outlet and put the tool bag in the plastic cubby on the side of the hatch area. She hooked up the compressor and started filling the tire. In under two minutes, Khloe unplugged the power cord, activated the hatch switch, flipped the air hose connection off the tire valve, and walked up to Audrey's side. "All done ma'am. Get that looked at soon as you can."

Audrey held out a twenty dollar bill. "Here, hon, take this."

Khloe turned and walked away. "No ma'am. Can't take that. You have yourself a great day."

Syd and Audrey now possessed two kilos of high grade heroin.

"Fantastic job, Khloe. You go, girl." Candy drove around the hospital to the main entrance and called Jamey.

"How's Gina?"

"She's fine. Baby's fine. Seven pounds, two ounces. I can't visit yet. They're telling me I can probably see her tomorrow. Won't be able to see the baby until Gina's released. What a day, huh?"

"Yeah. What a day. I'm glad Gina and the baby are doin' good. Hey, need you to do this for Gina and me. Call the state police anonymous drug enforcement hotline. You can Google it. Report a red Toyota Sienna van tag number CL 6969, Georgia plate. The van is being driven by a white middle aged couple. You saw them on parking lot four at Mountain View. They are drug traffickers moving large quantities of heroin. They have a juvenile who was abducted in Annapolis with them. Use the courtesy phone in the lobby, Jamey. You can watch what's happening from the rear second floor of the hospital. When the cops get there, they are going to take Lily to social services. She'll be safe. Gina can call them and get it straightened out. Call me when it's over with. You can meet us out front. You can squeeze in with us and ride back to my house. Stay with us tonight."

"I'm on it, Candy."

64

I Know

"I have to see Jo before we leave." Candy got a visitor's pass. Jo had been transferred to a private room. Her nurse told Candy she'd been through a terrible ordeal. Her body would heal soon. The psychological effects might linger.

"I am so glad you're OK, Jo. It's all over the news. Did they tell you? It was Erik Stryker's twin brother who hurt you."

"Yeah, I asked the police. Told me they were identical twins. I don't remember much of anything after he used that stun gun on me. They said I was drugged. I remember kicking the clothes dryer and seeing another woman on a mattress. They told me the other woman died. I was lucky that cop found me. My wrists and ankles are so sore, and you can see my mouth. Jo had been holding her hand across her throat as she talked. Candy tugged gently at her arm.

"Don't, Candy...please."

"Jo, I know." Candy let go and laid her hand on Jo's midsection and then moved her hand slowly... down.

"Don't, Candy...."

Candy pulled her hand away and stroked Jo's hair. "It's OK, Jo. I know. I've known all along. You are what's in here." Candy held her hand over her heart. "That's you. The rest is whatever you want it to be. I love you as you are or how you wanna be."

"How did you know, Candy? I'm so careful. People can be so cruel. I wasn't sure how you would react. It has been eating away at me. Wondering how it might affect us...you know?"

"It's not important, Jo, really. I'm more than OK with you as you are. Trust me."

Jo attempted a smile. The sides of her mouth were suffering

from being gagged. She reached for Candy's hand. "You're special, Candy, and you don't even know it."

"Does that mean you'll go shopping with me?"

"Well, maybe… so long as you don't pick up any cute young guys."

"Smart ass. Get better and come stay with me for a while. Take some time off."

"I'll do that. I promise."

65

It's Crime - It Doesn't Pay

Jim and his lawyer Janice met at his house. He had news for her and couldn't risk their conversation being overheard.

"I have the money."

"What money? I haven't even asked for a retainer. What are you talking about?"

"I did a construction job for an acquaintance and I was paid in cash. Lots of cash."

"And this job paid well enough that you can pay Bank Two back as well as any penalty and the EEOC fine, should that come about?"

"Yes. I can do it, Janice. I have enough. And I can pay you too. The EEOC case is being withdrawn by the plaintiff."

"Well that's good news, Jim. I wasn't notified. How did you find out?"

"The plaintiff advised me. She saw no justice being served by hurting me or my business. Her antagonist is, well, no longer part of the equation."

"I see. Interesting. Getting back to your cash on hand. I don't see how we can walk into Bank Two with that much cash. It sends up serious red flags. And you can't just deposit it without the same thing happening."

"What if you wrote a check and I gave you the cash, Janice. Would that work?"

"No. To use your cash, I'd have to wash it clean. That would be a crime of more magnitude than the one you're being charged with. There might be a solution. Whomever you 'rented' that big Cat to could sell it back to you for cash at a premium to sweeten the deal. You make any repairs and refurbish it to as-new condition.

Return it to inventory once inspected and approved by Bank Two. Pay an agreed upon fine. The cash is now the problem of the party you bought it from. And if you have any of that cash left over, I don't want to hear about it. I'll waive my fee on this for securing your future legal business."

"Wait, isn't Bank Two going to question how the loader just showed up?"

"Probably not, and if so, not for long. It's the right serial number and the right equipment. For them it's just a line item."

66

Unlikely Suspects

The red Toyota van was surrounded. The dispatch request was "every car available respond— drug dealers." Six officers crouched behind open vehicle doors. A megaphone message suggested that Syd and Audrey be smart and put their hands out their windows and surrender. They were patted down and cuffed without incident. They assumed the seat of shame on the median curb. Lily was put in the back of a patrol car occupied by a career social worker. She had experience with child abductions. Lily told the nice lady she was frightened. She said the police were scary. And Ms. Audrey and Mr. Syd were acting weird. She wanted to see her mommy.

The search of the van revealed two kilos of suspected heroin. The drugs were quickly located in a fabric tool bag found in the rear of the van. Syd and Audrey were read their rights, arrested, booked, and an initial appearance was held. They requested representation. They were denied bail.

Jamey had watched from the second floor of the hospital. He was relieved that Lily was in good hands. She'd be back with her mom soon. And that couple? They deserved whatever happened to them.

He called Gina. She was groggy and tired but happy. He could visit soon. He had to let her know what had happened.

"Gina, please listen to the whole story. You know Audrey and Syd have been skulking around. Lily and I were in reception and Candy got attacked. It was a wild scene. I was afraid guns would be drawn so I asked a woman if she would take Lily into the ladies' room for a few minutes until things calmed down. She took her in and it turned out it was Audrey. Candy helped me. I was panicking. She had a plan to take Audrey and Syd down. It worked. They won't be a problem anymore. They've been arrested. Lily is with social services. I'll give you a number to call. They won't release her to me, only you. I'm sorry to put this on you. She is safe .We'll all be together soon."

"It's OK, Jamey. I understand. I'll call social services right now. Guess you won't want to babysit for me anytime soon, huh?"

Jamey checked on Abe next. He was about to be transferred to a hospital in Nashville. He was stable. He'd need to have extensive surgeries. His skull would need to be pieced back together. His jawbone, nose, eye sockets, and mouth all would require surgery. The prognosis was poor. Abe's brain had bled and swelled. Brain damage was certain.

Jamey called Candy and gave her the good news regarding Syd and Audrey. Her plan worked perfectly. They no longer posed a threat. They were already behind bars. Gina was following up with social services to get Lily back. Candy asked him to meet them for the ride back to her house.

67

Stack For You, Stack For Me

Everyone was exhausted. Candy ordered pizza.

"Don't tell me how nice the house is, Jamey. I can't take any more of that. I actually didn't have much to do with it. Anybody want a beer?"

Jamey and Khloe sat on one side of the kitchen table. Scorp and Candy sat opposite. When they finished eating, Candy asked for her guests' attention.

"Khloe, we have four hundred thousand dollars downstairs waiting for you. And an extra hundred thousand for helping scam Syd and Audrey. My purple Challenger is yours if you want it. I tried to give it to Jim Griot but it was too girly for him. He said I looked better in it. I'm tired of the attention it draws. I can take the Accord. I'm giving the Odyssey to Gina. We're grateful for everything you've done for us."

"Jamey, we have four hundred seventy-five thousand dollars downstairs for you. And an extra hundred thousand to cover the delay and the fuckin' aggravation. The weapons we got out of Abe's truck and Scorp's weapons are gonna be scrapped. Except the TEC 5000 rifle. That's yours to keep if you want it. It's worth fifteen grand."

"We're gonna help with Abe's medical expenses. I never meant to hurt him that bad. I just wanted to stop him. He worked with Scorp for years without any problems, and we understand he was due the money. I talked to his social worker at Mountain View the last time I visited him, before they shipped him to Nashville. She was able to locate Abe's husband…er, partner. He told her he'll set up their house so he can care for Abe once he's home."

"Jo and Gina and her baby should be released tomorrow They're all moving in. You two can stay too … as long as you can stand me."

"All of the rest of the drugs are in burn barrels. Scorp is gonna light them up. We don't need the money we'd get from selling them. They'd just end up ruining people's lives or killing them. I'm not completely rehabbed. I'll be in the family room with a bottle of vodka for a while tonight if anyone cares to join me. If not, good night. All the bedrooms are open."

68

Closure Of Sorts

Bob and Bobby were slumped in the two new leather recliners Bob's wife just bought for them. They were enjoying the massage action, dual cup holders, triple USB ports, and cubbies to hold remotes that rounded out the creature comfort list. Bobby had cut his vacation short when Bob's heroics went viral.

"Bob, I sure missed out, huh? I take off and you end up a celebrity without me? Damn, brother, I'm jealous."

"I know you better than that, Bobby. You wouldn't want to have been anywhere near this one. I guarantee it. Unless you like lookin' at strangled dead women with burn marks."

"So, what does Corporal Creed say about the Erik Stryker case, Bob? Is it still a thing? I mean, is there anybody out there who cares what happened to him now?"

"I've turned the file over, Bobby. Michelle and Shannon have it. Erik could have been responsible for some of them murders. I heard the identical twin DNA match might fuck up the investigation. Thing is, I thought I was getting close to solving *his* murder. I mean, I had a woman who Tracy Lynne called Candy, had big tits and owned a purple Challenger and had a Jersey accent who was supposed to hook up with her in that trailer that night. Candy flakes out and the next thing you know Erik is dead fifty miles from his house behind that store. The owner of Club 654 sees two blondes, one of them matching the description of Candy, and the other a regular at the club named Jo Brooks, who always wears a red scarf, getting in a beige van with Erik the night he called out sick early and croaked. The trailer meth freak we found at the scene with his brother who can still mumble words says 'trailer-Tracy Lynne-big tits-party-Candy-chickens-spiders' to me at the hospital. Then maybe a couple days later I get a 911 about an armed robbery and there's a little woman named Candise with big ones sitting on the steps when I get there. Fuckin' mansion. So she says the guy at the bottom of the steps with his head split and his face kicked in held a shotgun and a machine pistol on her and she pushed him and he fell down the steps. I'm leaving the scene and I see a purple Challenger in her garage. Has black wheels like Tracy Lynne described. And then Candise, the name on her license, doesn't show up the next day at the station to file the formal report like she was supposed to. Her name, Candise, is surely long for Candy. To top it off, a mean lookin' man with his face and arms all bandaged up shows up at the scene with another woman. Course they're all friends. If somebody put a gun to my head I'd swear Candy and the woman with her that night had a part in what happened to Erik. I'm just saying, Bobby. Michelle and Shannon got all of this. It's up to them now. With Erik and Quinn dead and the serial murders near solved, is it really worth going after whoever killed Erik?"

"Well, when you put it that way, no."

Bob's wife hollered down from the kitchen. "Turn on channel six!"

Channel Six's news van was parked in front of the Stryker house. Their investigative reporter was interviewing Daisy Turnbuckle. Daisy was explaining what an important role she played in the capture of Quinn Stryker. If not for her, he'd still be free, killing women at will.

"Damn, Bob. Creed should hire her to replace you when you retire. It's still happening in two weeks, right?"

"Yep, two weeks. Until then I'm runnin' radar out on 43 and drinkin' coffee. You planning on visiting us in Florida?"

"You bet."

Bob arrowed down. "Let's watch some reruns of Blue Bloods and knock back a few."

69

Loose Ends

Gina was released from Mountain View. She and Jamey had decided on a name. She would be known as Breeze Jamie Lamartina. Gina, Breeze, Lily and Jamey moved in. Gina'd explained the fiasco at the hospital when Lily was abducted to social services to their satisfaction. They had a mini suite on the third floor of Candy's house to themselves. Candy spent an afternoon with Gina soon after they moved in. They talked about their relationship and how so much had changed since their time together in Annapolis. Gina explained that she was in love and determined to be faithful to Jamey. Candy said she understood and professed her support. The strain of the conversation was evident. They shared memories and parted with hugs and tears.

Candy picked Jo up from Mountain View when she got the green light to go home. Jo took one of the larger bedrooms on the second floor overlooking a clearing and woods toward the rear of the property.

Scorp was pain and bandage free. He resumed his running regimen and hit the weight room he'd installed behind the garage. When he felt grouchy he slept in the small bedroom next to the gym. Khloe was looking into options for the plastic surgery she'd talked him into.

Khloe interviewed and was hired at Mountain View. She sold her condo. Her mother was coming to visit soon. She was in the second floor bedroom with the large sitting room attached. She'd had it soundproofed at Scorp's request.

Jim Griot managed to avoid jail time and save Essential Sales & Rental with the help of his new co-owner Janice Barnes. He hired a new office manager. He'd paid off Sunset Assisted Living and moved his parents to a small family-owned facility. They were doing better there.

Winter had arrived. Candy was surprised at how cold it got in Tennessee. She wasn't expecting some nights dipping down to twenty degrees. She was watching deer strip bark off saplings. A courier parked and sprinted up the front steps. He had a letter for Scorpion at this address. She met him at the front door and let him through.

"Hey Scorp. Letter for you. You gotta sign for it."

"Humph … be right there." It was a standard letter size envelope. Scorp ripped it open. There was a small folded piece of paper inside. He unfolded it. In bold type, it read **"29 stop complete thx."** He stuffed it in his pocket. His twenty-nine million dollar payment for the stolen cars was deposited in his offshore account.

Candy and Scorp joined Khloe in the kitchen. Khloe picked up the remote to turn the news off when she saw Scorp. Candy grabbed her arm. "Wait, look!" The breaking news banner flashed across the screen:

Annapolis couple sentenced to thirty years for drug trafficking and kidnapping a minor.

Candy's cell dinged. It was her doctor. Her latest lab test results showed improvement. Her HIV was not detectable. Her liver functions were normal, indicating her Hepatitis C infection was under control. Jo had pushed her to seek treatment. Her upper tooth still needed attention. It had been loose since her encounter with Sam and Dave. She had an appointment scheduled. Dr. David Haspert was on site temporarily at his new office that just opened nearby. The billboard out on 64 announced he was offering discounts on cosmetic procedures. She couldn't wait to see him.

Scorp decided he would turn the bitcoin room over to Jo. He'd never understood it and didn't particularly care for the idea of digital anything, much less digital cash. And Jo "knew a guy." Her guy spent a few weeks working with her cleaning up the operation. He was impressed with the quality of the installation. The HVAC system was state of the art. There were underground diesel generators out back that were automatically started during a power failure. He saw plans in a folder for solar arrays that could one day be utilized. He showed Jo the one-month average value. It was sixteen million U.S. Jo would be responsible for payment of the substantial electric bill.

Michelle Wright and Shannon Dorsey concluded the Stryker serial murder cases. Although it was never determined which brother killed two of the women, forensic evidence exposed that they were both responsible in the rest of the murders Having closed the case, they were reviewing cases that had been neglected. The Erik Stryker file intrigued them, possibly because of who he was and what he had done. They decided it warranted a review. Over lunch, the detectives delved into the case interviews. That afternoon inquiries they made showed Sam and Dave were deceased and Tracy Lynne had moved to Florida. Candise Doubleday and Jo Brooks rose to the top of their person of interest list.

Candy opened the front door. Scorp had decided the remote-controlled entrance gates were not worth the effort so they just left the gates open at all times now. The two female detectives were taken aback by Candy's stunning smile. She welcomed them in. They joined Jo and Candy in the formal living room.

"Thanks for meeting with us today, ladies. Detective Wright and I have a few questions for you regarding your whereabouts on the night Erik Stryker was beaten to death." Shannon opened a file and showed them the crime scene photos.

"We have a witness putting you both outside Club 654 that night. The witness also said Erik got into a van outside the club with both of you."

Candy answered. "Well, that's true. We did get in my van with Erik. We didn't even know his name." Candy looked down and the detectives could see she was embarrassed. Her shoulders slumped, she sucked in a breath, and her cheeks flushed.

Jo put her hand on Candy's shoulder to comfort her. "We'd been doing shots of vodka that night. Candy was new in town at the time and we…well…we fucked Erik in the van. Not to be crude…. To be specific, I sucked him and Candy fucked him. It's not something we do, you know…on the regular…it just happened. He was super cute and we were super drunk. We took him home after that." He told us his brother had the Jeep they shared and he needed a ride." Michelle and Shannon were stifling smiles.

Michelle cleared her throat. "Just one more question should wrap this up." She turned to Candy. "Did you drive to a country store out on rural road 38 in a purple Dodge Challenger?"

"I did. I'm new here and I was looking for some nice country roads to drive my car on. I remember driving on 38 and stopping at a store. I needed to pee and get some Newports. I smoked a lot at the time. The restroom was disgusting. I couldn't even use it. And there was this really old woman with no teeth behind the counter who was staring at me, and a girl with saucers for eyes trying to flirt with me on the lot when I went to get back in the car. She kept asking me what my name was. I got the fuck out of there as fast as I could. That was the first time I went anywhere around here except Piggly Wiggly."

Michelle and Shannon noticed. Candy had shed one single tear.

"That's a shame that was one of your first impressions of our state, Ms. Doubleday. Well, that's all we needed. We'll be on our way. Thanks so much for your time."

Michelle and Shannon smirked when they reached the car. "Shannon, that wasn't worth doing except for the exceptional entertainment value. Between Bob's undecipherable chicken scratch file notes and that fabulous follow up interview, there's only one place for this case. The trash can."

When they returned to their offices, Corporal Creed summoned them. "I have some good news for you. You've both been accepted for that pilot management position up in Nashville." Michelle and Shannon high fived. They would likely be the first African American lesbian couple to lead a team of homicide detectives. They were confident their performance would make their shared post permanent.

Candy called a house meeting. It would take place at eleven on Saturday morning. Khloe would be free from her hospital duties that day. Special guest would be Janice Barnes, principal at Barnes & Co. and co-owner of Essential Sales & Rental. She was asked to attend and listen. They were to let her know what their aspirations entailed. She would then act as a consultant and provide legal advice.

Candy took the floor first. She thanked everyone for attending and introduced Janice Barnes to the group. Jim Griot had asked Janice to attend as a favor to him after Candy called him asking for a good attorney. Janice tried not to stare. Four gorgeous young women held her attention. She felt her face flush.

"My name is Candy. My wish is to start up a drug addiction rehab center right here in town. I want a decent facility, an honest staff and no bullshit sessions sucking money from parents. The budget is ten million start up. I need help buying shit…er the building, hiring, managing, everything. I only know the business from the patient side."

"Hi, Janice." Gina and Jamey were next. Gina spoke. "Our wish is to set up a chain of first class daycare centers. The budget is ten million with substantial additional cash available. We need help with liability insurance, financing, employee standards and benefits, cash flow projections and such. So, we need help with a business plan.

"Hi, Janice. I'm Jo. I wish to establish the Great Smoky Mountain Community Center for LGBTQ individuals. It would offer counseling, employment and housing assistance and have an accredited surgeon available for consultation. My budget is seven million to start. I need help creating a non-profit to run the facility.

Scorp raised his hand.

"My name is Scorp, Ms. Barnes. I'm hopin' to help build up and put up money for a string of shelters for abused women. Hire up people who know what the fuck they're doing. My budget is…well…big. I need help with just about everything. It doesn't need to make money. I've done enough of that."

Khloe was the last to speak. "Hi, Ms. Barnes. I'm Khloe. I'm an RN and work at Mountain View. My wish is to establish a burn unit at Mountain View. My budget is limited but I'm pretty convincing." She looked over at Scorp. "I need help with fundraising."

Janice Barnes stood up and applauded. "Well, I must say, I thought I was on Shark Tank. I will assist everyone here to the best of my ability. I must admit I was skeptical when Jim asked me to come to this meeting. I'm nothing of the sort now. You should all be proud. You are all giving back at an age where most are not. I'll get to work and have recommendations in a month. In the meantime, I wish you all the best. Thanks so much for including me." Candy walked her out to her limo.

"So. Scorp, what did you think?" Candy was curious.

"Humph…She wasn't blowin' smoke up our asses."

70

Contentment

Candy threw her puffer jacket on. She poured herself a short Grey Goose, opened the sliding glass door softly, and shuffled out onto the bedroom balcony. The bare trees were swaying and early snow flurries swarmed furiously around her. She'd entertained Lily and Breeze all day while Gina and Jamey toured wedding venues. Candy had never been this happy. She had a family. Her new family filled her heart and her home. She'd finally succeeded. Finishing her drink, she slipped silently back inside, heeled her boots off, and shed her clothes. She lifted the quilt covered sheet, sliding across the silk. Jo stirred. Parted lip kisses. Candy pressed Jo's shoulder down as she climbed on top and guided her… in.

The next morning Jo and Candy watched from one of the front balconies. Down below, Scorp and Khloe were making their way to the Challenger. They were leaving to pick up Scorp's new Suburban. Candy thought Khloe looked perfect in her old car.

Scorp looked up, waved, and smiled.

Candy shouted out. "Drive safe! No texting! No hand held phones!"

About the author

Jake Lynchpin, Jr., drives the bus for the Thirty-Second First Revival Church, located in his home town of Chattahoochee, Tennessee. He wrote, edited, and published *Hooked Up*, Books 1 and 2, during his time waiting for the weekly Senior Sunday School classes to dismiss. Named "Most likely to succeed" in middle school, Jake has earned the "Bus Driver of the Year" award too many times to count. Jake lives with his mother, six dogs, and currently eighteen cats. He is frequently spotted at local yard sales and flea markets.